HAUNTED GUNSLINGER

James Johnson, illegitimate son of the legendary Wyatt Earp, moves to Wichita, Kansas for a fresh start. He brings his mother and his mentally disabled friend, Carson, with him. But fresh starts bring new problems.

Each year, on the same date, a gunslinger ghost shoots up Main Street at high noon. The apparition replays its last moments alive. The townsfolk believe the legendary spirit to be a residual haunt. Until the gunslinger finds a way to finally win a shootout.

Can James and Carson defeat the Haunted Gunslinger before more innocents die? Or will the Devil win the West?

Supernatural spirits can be deadly gunfighters…

This is a creepy tale of supernatural horror.

Haunted Gunslinger is the second novel in the *Son of Earp* series by Chuck Buda.

ALSO BY CHUCK BUDA

Gushers Series
The First Cut
Slashing Away
Tourniquet

The Debt Collector Series
Pay Up and Die
Delinquent
Bankrupt

Son of Earp Series
Curse of the Ancients
Haunted Gunslinger
Summoner of Souls

Visit my website to find all these books, and more!
www.authorchuckbuda.com

HAUNTED GUNSLINGER

CHUCK BUDA

This book is a work of fiction. Names, characters, places, and incidents either are the product of the author's imagination or are used fictitiously and any resemblance to actual persons, living or dead, business establishments, events, or locales is entirely coincidental.

HAUNTED GUNSLINGER
Copyright © 2016 by Chuck Buda
Edited by Jenny Adams
ISBN: 978-1535258159
www.authorchuckbuda.com

All rights reserved. No part of this book may be reproduced or transmitted in any form or by any means, electronic or mechanical, including photocopying, recording, or by any information storage and retrieval system, without permission in writing from the author, except by a reviewer who may quote brief passages in review.

Cover art © 2016 by Phil Yarnall | SMAYdesign.com
Interior design by Dullington Design Co.

The author greatly appreciates you taking the time to read his work. Please consider leaving a review wherever you bought this book or telling your friends or blog readers about this book to help spread the word.

Thank you for supporting my work. Without you the story would not be told.

Dedicated to my father for exposing me to the Wild West.

HAUNTED GUNSLINGER

PRELUDE

Sammy Tucker tripped over his own two feet and sprawled across the porch. He narrowly missed Jeanette Harper and the horse trough in front of the haberdashery. Jeanette gasped at the near collision and then went about her business when she realized it was Sammy. Several men across the street enjoyed a good laugh at Sammy's expense. He stood up and dusted himself off. Then he straightened his hat and strolled off down the street, pretending as though nothing had happened.

The daily bustle continued throughout the town. Folks were chatting and buying groceries at Miller's. The hot morning sun brought sweat stains to just about everybody's clothing. Everyone except Mrs. Donovan, of course. She waddled down the center of Main Street with her lilac parasol shading her chubby face. Her maize-colored skirt glided along the dusty road behind her. She wore her white gloves, regardless of the heat, because it would be uncivilized to appear in public less formally. She kept her nose in the air lest she breathe in the horse droppings that spotted the town.

The bell tower chimed twelve o'clock, signaling noon time to the residents of Wichita.

A gun shot rang out.

A few women leaving Miller's screamed. They dropped their parcels of sundries and skittered into the haberdashery. Mrs. Donovan wasted no time either. She flung her parasol and rolled across the street until she made it into Clip's Barber Shop. Jeanette Harper rounded the building for the safety of the alleyway.

Wesley Masterton dropped behind a rain barrel and pulled his six-shooter from its holster. He cocked the hammer and peered up the street. Besides the townspeople running to and fro along the sidewalks, the street was empty.

Another gunshot sounded. A puff of smoke drifted slowly along Main Street as the heat tried to drag it down.

Sammy Tucker screamed out as the slug entered his leg. He was sprinting up the street when the second shot connected with his hamstring. Sammy grabbed the back of his leg and crawled on his belly for the tavern. It was at least fifty yards from where he lie but it was his closest option for cover. Sammy cried from the pain of the hot lead, a streak of dirty tears running down his cheeks.

A third shot was fired. As the wisp of gun powder floated, Sheriff Axl Morgan charged out into the street. His rifle was drawn and his dark eyes surveyed the landscape for the shooter. A quiet calm settled in. Folks were no longer screaming or shouting, preferring not to give up their hiding spots.

The sheriff noticed a hazy image that hovered near the center of town, right in the middle of the street. He narrowed his eyes to focus on the oddity. It appeared to be the form of a man, yet Sheriff Morgan could see right through him. Morgan raised his rifle to sight in the gunslinger, only to find an apparition where the man was last standing. He lowered his head so the brim of his white hat would eliminate the sun's glare from the barrel. But it didn't help. The apparition stood in the middle of the road with its gun drawn.

Morgan cocked the lever of the rifle. Before he could squeeze off a round, another shot fired from the ghost's weapon. The bullet found its mark in Sheriff Axl Morgan's shoulder, narrowly missing his chest. The impact of the shot sent the sheriff flying backwards. He dropped his rifle and clutched his wound, after hitting the dirt. Blood flowed through his fingertips as he attempted to put pressure on the hole.

The gunslinger ghost laughed out loud in a sinister, evil fashion. It fired two more rounds down the street which danced up pebbles as they landed. The twisted laugh faded into the humid air along with the form of the shooter. A sense of peace came over the town and folks began to poke their heads back up to see what had happened.

Sheriff Morgan rolled onto his side to look for help. The blood from his shoulder slowed to a trickle. But he was very much in pain. The men who had laughed at Sammy Tucker crossed the street to attend to the sheriff. They helped him up and carried him to Doc Stinson's. As they went, the men asked Morgan if he had seen what they did. The sheriff replied that he hadn't seen anything, which was why he got shot.

Jeanette Harper and Ed Miller ran to Sammy Tucker. He had balled himself into a fetal position with one hand grabbing his leg wound. The tears that streaked his face made him look like the saddest or dirtiest clown ever seen. Jeanette felt sorry for the clumsy man now that he had been shot. She stroked his greasy hair and told him he would be okay.

Ed Miller checked the wound and declared the bullet had passed straight through the side of his thigh. He told Sammy he would live but Sammy just buried his face in Jeanette Harper's bosom and cried more emphatically. He liked the attention he was getting for the first time in his life. And he loved the smell of Jeanette's powdery breasts. He thought he might as well milk the moment for what it was worth. Pun intended, he smirked gently beneath his cries.

With the shooting finished, the townspeople congregated in the street to compare notes on what they had seen or thought they had seen. Everyone was stunned that a ghost had appeared in their quaint little town. Not just a ghost, but a ghost that could shoot a gun and harm living people. Women started saying prayers to protect themselves from the evil spirits. Men cussed in circles about the work of the devil. They wondered aloud about how they might try to protect their families.

Mayor Tom Samuels ran his sweaty hands through his long gray hair before replacing his hat on his head. He thought to himself, he wouldn't have believed it if he hadn't seen it with his own blue eyes. He had seen the ghost gunslinger before. He knew who the man was, at least when he was alive. The ghost was Francis Dodson, sure as shootin', he thought to himself. The mayor recognized the hazy face as clearly as if the man were still among the living. But he didn't want the people of town to panic. If they believed they had seen a ghost, folks might move out of town and take their votes with them.

CHAPTER 1

James swung the door open and entered the room. He went straight for the wash basin to clean the dirt from his hands before eating lunch.

"Hi, Mom. Hey, Carson."

"Hello, James. You're home a few minutes early." Sarah, James' mother, sat at the table sipping a cup of tea. She lowered the cup and peered at James with her crystal-blue eyes.

"Yeah, I ran home because I am so hungry I could eat two horses." James ruffled Carson's hair with his wet hands. Carson shot James an angry look and then, just as quickly, smiled that his best friend was home from work. "Mr. Miller let me go a few minutes early too, on account of my quickness with stacking the bags of feed."

James fixed himself a sandwich of apple butter and cheese. As he put the pieces together, Carson left the table to follow closely behind James. The older boy didn't mind the younger shadow. He enjoyed Carson's company and looked upon him as a little brother, rather than a friend.

"Would you mind heating me another tea, dear? I keep feeling a draft from the hallway."

"Sure, Mom." James set the tea pot on the small, cast iron stove. He almost stepped on Carson when he turned around. Then he hurried to the table to eat his sandwich. Carson followed James to the table. "Wanna know what I heard at the store?" James tore a piece of his sandwich off and handed it to Carson, who cheerfully took a bite.

"Is it appropriate for the audience? I don't want you to tell another story about Sammy Tucker's restroom habits at the table." Sarah rested her head on her hands.

"Naw, nothing like that." James reddened. "Anyway, I heard Mrs. Donovan complaining to Mr. Miller about the high-noon-shooter. And everybody in town is worried he will come back again this year." James spoke with a huge ball of sandwich in his cheek.

"What is a nooner-shooter?" Carson imitated James with a lump of sandwich stuffed in his cheek.

"Not a nooner-shooter. A high-noon-shooter. Apparently, each year on June 22nd, a ghost appears in the middle of town and shoots off its gun." James paused to observe his mother's reaction. She tilted her head at James, as if he were making up a silly tale. Carson soaked it all in. He stopped chewing the sandwich and stared at James with wide open eyes. "Honest. I heard Mrs. Donovan say the first time it happened Sheriff Morgan and Sammy Tucker got shot." Carson swallowed the lump of sandwich whole with a loud gulp.

"Don't you think it's just a tall tale to entertain people?" Sarah chided James for believing such a far-fetched story. She raised her arms to fix the braid in her long, black hair.

"Mr. Miller said it really happened but that Mayor Samuels insists it never happened, even though everyone in town witnessed it." James couldn't hide the excitement in his voice. "The 22nd is tomorrow and I can't wait to see what happens."

Sarah tsked out loud. She rolled her eyes and moved to the stove to pour herself some tea. "I don't think it is real. And even if it were real, I think you have had enough supernatural adventures to last a lifetime." She shot a glance at Carson, who didn't pick up on her reference to the battle with Crouching Bear.

James watched Carson's face to make sure he didn't realize what they were talking about. He was relieved to see Carson had now occupied himself with stealing another piece of James' sandwich.

James smiled to himself that Carson had a big appetite for such a small boy. "Well, I don't think I could do anything about it anyway. I just want to see it for myself."

"I want to see it for myself, too." Carson spoke through a new lump of sandwich in his cheek. James patted Carson's shoulder.

"I won't let you see it since you will be home for lunch. I'll make a nice, thick soup so you have to sit in here and eat slowly. That way you won't have time to wander around the streets while this ghost legend is showing itself." She poured her tea and then took a small sip. "Now, if you'll excuse me, I have to get back downstairs and see how the preparations are coming along. No rest for the madam." Sarah kissed James' forehead and then left the room.

When they had moved from Iowa to Wichita, Sarah landed the madam job at the brothel. She had told James she wanted to quit the business and start over. But when they had arrived in Wichita, the only open position at that time was for a new madam. Lady Brodsky had passed away from a long bout with syphilis. And the rest of the girls in the brothel were too young or inexperienced to run the show. So Sarah was hired on the spot and she was finally able to quit the working side of the business.

James looked down at his plate and realized Carson had eaten almost his entire sandwich. He was so excited about the ghost gunslinger he had filled his mouth with words instead of bread. He smiled at Carson and then rose to make himself another sandwich. While he fixed the next one, Carson issued a loud burp behind him. James laughed out loud, which got Carson laughing too.

"What do you think the shooter looks like? I'll bet he is all white and mean looking. He probably has black eyes." James leaned across the table to imitate a scary ghost as he returned to the table. Carson's eyes opened wide and he leaned back in his chair to distance himself from the image.

"I don't want to see the nooner-shooter. He scares me."

"Aw, you've never seen him, Carson. Besides, I got you covered. You know I would protect you from anyone, including evil spirits." James raised his hands above his head to simulate a monster grabbing the young boy. Carson got up and ran out of the room, screaming all the way down the hall. James laughed to himself and took another bite of his sandwich. As he chewed, he heard his mother scream up the stairs.

"JAMES!"

"Uh-oh." James swallowed the lump of sandwich and then quickly cleaned up after himself. He stuffed the uneaten portion of the sandwich into his shirt pocket and then raised the bedroom window. He heard his mother's stomping feet coming down the hall toward the room. James swung his legs out the window and closed it behind him. He would have to slide down the porch post to escape his mother's anger.

CHAPTER 2

"Ain't no such thing as ghosts. It's hogwash." Mayor Tom Samuels slammed his shot glass down on the table. It was late afternoon and the saloon was slowly filling up as the town finished working for the day. Once he overheard men discussing the gunslinger ghost at a nearby table, he decided he couldn't keep his opinions to himself. He was afraid people would panic again. Each year, the town's reaction grew.

Randall Gilbert stared at the Mayor. "You seen it yerself. Them boys was shot clear as day."

A small crowd had formed around the Mayor's table, as patrons sensed the ensuing debate.

The Mayor rubbed his gray goatee and shook his head. He poured himself another whiskey and looked around at the faces in the crowd. "People were scared for no good reason. So they shot around the streets blindly. That's how those men got hurt." He lied easily, as political life had prepared him for it for decades. He downed another drink and pursed his lips at the burn going down his throat.

"Now look here, Tom. We all seen what happened with our own eyes. That ghost done shot up the town hisself, and you know it."

"That's Mayor to you, Philip." The Mayor glared at the lanky man hovering over him. "And don't tell me what I saw. You were there. I was there. Most of us were there. The excitement messed with folks' minds. Somebody went off half-cocked and fired their gun, which sent everyone running and shooting. Of course, somebody was bound to get hurt." He looked around at all the disbelieving faces. "Then you all sat around like a bunch of old hens, spinning a yarn to fix everyone's britches into a knot."

"If we is all making it up, then how come it happens every year at the same time?" Randall Gilbert challenged the Mayor.

Mayor Samuels poured another drink. His hand was starting to shake as the whiskey accumulated in his blood. He watched his fat fingers as they grasped the shot glass. The argument was getting to him and he wanted to regain control of his emotions and the situation before things got out of hand. He let go of the shot glass and reached into his jacket for a cigarette. As he licked paper and stuck it between his lips, the Mayor made eye contact with Gilbert. Philip struck a match on the table and fired up the Mayor's cigarette.

"Thank you, Philip." The Mayor nodded at the man and breathed smoke through his hairy nostrils. "All I am saying is that we need to stay calm so nobody else gets hurt." His voice was serene and the angst in the crowd was soothed into silence. "I, personally, don't believe in ghosts. That's not to say that they don't exist. However, we owe it to each other to look out for one another. We have wives and children to think of. We have livelihoods to protect. And, if everyone runs through the streets hollering and shooting, we stand to lose more than we gain."

Some of the men nodded, in understanding if not in agreement with the Mayor. A few others peeled away from the crowd, whispering as they left. Those that remained looked to the Mayor for more guidance.

As he took the cigarette from his lips, an ash tumbled down his black coat. Mayor Samuels downed another shot and made eye contact with each of the men surrounding his table. He smiled internally at his ability to turn an argument in his favor. His skills had served him well, in gaining office and in keeping him from getting punched out as a youngster.

"I will personally guarantee there will be no ghostly troubles tomorrow. I will walk out into the middle of the street, at high noon, and show everyone there is nothing to be scared of. You have my word on it." The Mayor nodded emphatically to put an exclamation point on his promise.

Several men whistled their shock while a low rumble of excitement worked through the crowd. The Mayor overheard a few comments like "he's crazier than a long-tailed cat in a room full of rocking chairs" and "don't he know he's fixin' ta die" and "that's why he's Mayor of this here town." He grinned with confidence at the men and placed the cigarette back into his lips. Then he ordered up a round of whiskeys on himself to a pleasing bunch of cheers and claps. The crowd dispersed as the men scooted to the bar to collect their free drinks.

Mayor Samuels kept the grin on his face but he was shaking inside. He did what he had to in order to maintain control of his town. But deep down he knew the ghost was real. He had seen it with his own eyes, too. And he was scared to death of what he had promised the folks. He gulped the huge lump that formed in his throat and reached for the bottle with a shaking hand. The Mayor snatched up the bottle quickly before anybody could see his fear and he poured a large drink. The neck of the bottle clinked the glass several times, as his hand continued to shake. Luckily, nobody noticed as the saloon had returned to regular festivities and loud banter.

The Mayor admonished himself for making such a wild claim as taunting the apparition. His mind flipped through an inventory of possible excuses to recuse him of his promise before high noon. But he knew he had to go through with it, for the good folks of his town. He loved this town and most of the people who lived here. His political aspirations aside, he really had enjoyed building this small town into the hub of businesses that it had become. And he would do anything to protect these good people. Even if it meant he had to die to do it.

Philip slapped the Mayor on the back as he went to a table in the back corner of the saloon. Mayor Samuels smiled up at him and winked to show his mirth and confidence. The men bought it, for now, he whispered to himself. He glanced around the bar and drained the glass. The burn of the alcohol flaming his throat and then his gut. He crushed out the butt of his cigarette on the floor and began praying to God to save his soul. The Mayor wanted to make his peace in case he succumbed to the ghostly gunslinger tomorrow afternoon.

CHAPTER 3

James was stocking a shelf with bars of soap. The cheap ones had no smells whatsoever. The more expensive ones had nice fragrances that brought to mind sun-washed fields or flower gardens. He liked to sniff the soaps before stacking them on the shelves. Of course, he made sure to look around before smelling them to make sure that nobody watched him.

The chime above the door jingled as a new customer entered the general store. The store was named Miller's after the proprietor, Mr. Miller. Ed Miller. James liked Mr. Miller. He was an older gentleman with a horse-shoe shaped patch of gray hair around his shiny bald head. Mr. Miller was tall and thin, but exceptionally stronger than he appeared. James had struggled lifting a crate of fruits one time and Mr. Miller had come to his aid. Rather than grabbing one side of the container to help James, Mr. Miller hoisted the crate up onto the counter himself. And James had noticed the man didn't even strain or grunt to do it.

"Good day, Edwin."

"Well, good day to you, Mrs. Walsh. You look lovely as usual. What can I do for you today?" Mr. Miller was successful for more reasons than being the only store in town. He knew how to extend the highest levels of courtesy and service to his customers.

James stopped listening to their exchange as he bent to grab more bars of soap. He sniffed the bars while he was squatted down to avoid detection. As he was about to rise and continue stacking, he overheard Mrs. Walsh mention the name "Earp." His ears immediately pricked up and he rose to pay closer attention over the shelves.

"Why, he did so much to clean up the hooligans in this town but I wonder if he could have done anything about that dreadful ghost." Mrs. Walsh spoke with her hand resting on her fair cheek.

"Well, I don't know what a man can do against an other-worldly spirit, Mrs. Walsh. But I certainly felt safer with Wyatt Earp as marshal over Sheriff Morgan." Mr. Miller saw James watching them. "Do you need help, James?"

"Uh, no, sir. I couldn't help but hear you talking about Wyatt Earp. Did you say he was sheriff here?" James felt the excitement swelling in his gut.

"Yes, but what does that have to do with stocking the shelves? I don't pay you to stand around and talk, you know." He smiled back at Mrs. Walsh and continued their conversation.

James dropped the bars of soap back into the crate and walked around the shelf. As he approached the counter, Mr. Miller was laughing about a story from the past. The story involved Wyatt Earp cleaning out the saloon single-handedly. Apparently, two men had gotten into an argument over who was going to buy a patch of land just outside of town. One thing led to another and the men began fighting. However, as the brawl ensued, several other men got stepped on or shoved by the fighting men. Soon thereafter, the fight escalated to about ten men. And it seemed that Wyatt Earp beat all ten men into submission, several with his famed pistol-whipping. James was delighted with the tale and let out a loud and drawn out, "Whoa."

"James, I told you to finish stacking the soap. There are a lot more things that need to be shelved and I can't have you standing around. Now get back to work." Mr. Miller got irritated and the wrinkles on his bald head stacked up as his eyebrows came together in anger.

"Sorry, Mr. Miller. I just love to read or hear about Wyatt Earp. He is a hero of mine and I just can't help myself."

"Well, I don't know if I would call him a hero." Mr. Miller straightened up. "He was a fine marshal and kept folks safe but he had his moments. The man knew how to live it up and he probably caused as many problems as he solved."

"And he was quite a character with the ladies, too." Mrs. Walsh blushed. She moved the hand from her cheek and patted her handbag in embarrassment of her affection for the legend.

"I wish I could meet him someday. I've learned so much about him and I would love to get to know my fa…, uh, my famous hero. I, uh, should get back to work on those soap bars, I guess. Sorry, Mr. Miller. Sorry, Ma'am." James backed away and hurried to the crate of soap. He had narrowly missed slipping up. His mother had warned him not to mention Wyatt Earp was his father since it might attract attention.

"What a nice young man. I haven't seen him before. What is his name?"

"James. James Johnson. He came into town about a week ago with his mother and a little brother. He's been a big help since joining us here in the store. But, sometimes, he needs to concentrate better on his work." Mr. Miller glowered over his nose in James' direction. James smiled and waved a bar of soap before placing it on the shelf. He got away with one this time but he had to be more careful in the future.

James' mind wandered while he worked. His thoughts bounced between his mother and Carson, and the stories of his legendary father. He was happy they had moved from Iowa to Kansas. It had given them a fresh start and they were doing better here. He had a job. His mother had a better position so she didn't have to whore anymore. And Carson seemed happier in the new place. It was easier for Carson to forget that his mother was "away" with relatives since he didn't have all the old reminders that existed in Iowa. He still asked James when she was coming home, but the questions were less frequent since they had moved. James hoped to hide Carson's mother's passing from him for as long as he could. Hopefully, forever. Carson was slow so he might be able to pull it off. Sometimes he felt guilty about hiding the facts from Carson, but he knew it was best for his little friend, to protect his fragile mind.

James sighed out loud, which drew the attention of Mrs. Walsh and Mr. Miller. He nodded and smiled and they went back to conversing. James wondered what the ghost gunslinger looked like. Was it fully visible? Or was it white like they described in those scary chapbooks? Could a ghost really shoot a gun with real bullets? Or was it all make believe as Mayor Samuels touted? James was fascinated with this story and he couldn't wait to find out more about it tomorrow at noon. He smiled to himself, as he daydreamed about a possible new adventure.

CHAPTER 4

Carson giggled while he watched James' expression sink. James couldn't believe he had been bested, yet again, by Carson's skills with cards. He slapped the table and pushed his chair back to stand. Carson collected the cards and began to shuffle for another game.

"I told you to pay attention." Carson grinned from ear to ear with satisfaction. James shot Carson a look of frustration and then turned to grab a mug of water from the counter.

"I did pay attention. I always pay attention. I swear, one of these days I will beat you at poker and I will dance around you in celebration when it happens."

Carson kept shuffling. James gulped down the water and then walked over to the window. The night sky appeared as a translucent, deep blue with the full moon rising. He breathed in the crisp air as he watched some party-goers walk towards the saloon. James appreciated the fact he and Carson were able to eat and play cards in the room. He didn't miss the long nights on the porch back in Iowa. He did miss their favorite hiding spot though.

"I wonder what the gunslinger will look like." James' mind forwarded to the much-anticipated sighting. In fifteen hours, he would know whether the legend was true or not.

Carson paused and stared at James' back as he continued to stare out the window. "I bet he will be whited and creepy."

James turned to face Carson. "You mean white, not whited." James approached the table and sat down. "And you're just repeating what I said yesterday. I have to see it but Mr. Miller and Mom might try to stop me."

Carson looked confused. James continued anyway.

"I heard Mr. Miller and Mrs. Walsh today at the store." James leaned across the table and spoke in a hushed voice as if to avoid detection. "They said Wyatt Earp was here in town a few years ago and he busted men up. But he left town before the appearance of the ghost."

Carson swallowed loudly and hung on every word with wide eyes.

"Don't you see? This is my chance to outdo my father." James looked for recognition in Carson's face but found nothing. "I've always wanted to follow in my daddy's footsteps, but, this time, I have a chance to do one better."

Carson blinked at James. James sighed and put his head in his hands, elbows resting on the table. He loved Carson like his little brother but sometimes it was difficult to communicate with him.

"I can make a legend of my own if I can figure out how to get rid of this ghostly gunslinger."

Carson nodded in understanding. Finally, James thought to himself.

"But I thought we were going to do adventures together." Carson emphasized the "together" with a hurtful whine.

"Oh yeah. Of course. We will both go on lots of adventures. But this one might be too…well, I mean, I wouldn't want you to get hurt, buddy." James tried to convey his worry for Carson without crushing his hopes for fighting evil with James. "A ghost might be too scary for you. But I know you could whoop a whole saloon full of cattle thieves and cheaters."

Carson sat up straight with pride. He seemed satisfied that James would include him in taking out the bad guys.

James rubbed his temples. He struggled to figure out how he could help the town with the gunslinger. It would be difficult since he didn't know what it looked like or where in the street it would show up. And he just didn't know enough about the history of the legend. Who was the gunslinger? Had he lived in this town in the past? What was the significance of the date and time that it appeared? James had so many questions and not enough answers.

"It's going to be difficult tomorrow. Mr. Miller already warned me, if I was going to come home for lunch, like I normally do, he would make me leave the store early to avoid noon hour. And Mom said if I came home for lunch, she would make me eat a long, slow lunch so I would be stuck here in the room at the same time. I'm trapped on both ends." He looked at the ceiling in search of a solution.

"Maybe you can left the store early and then don't come home on time." Carson spoke while he flipped cards over on the table. The first card was the one-eyed Jack. The second card was a four of clubs.

"You're a genius, Carson." Carson beamed at the high praise. "You figured it out. I will leave early to come home for lunch just like Mr. Miller said. But, on my way home, I might just find myself getting carried away with something that keeps me from getting here. That way I can watch for the gunslinger and figure out how to defeat him." James slammed his fists down on the table in excitement. "Then I'm on my way to becoming a legend like my old man." He was ecstatic with the possibilities.

Carson shuffled the cards quickly and then stared at James as if to plead for another game. James nodded and Carson started dealing happily. James lost himself in thought, trying to determine the best vantage point for the noon-time shoot out. He knew being anywhere in the street was dangerous. And he wouldn't be able to watch from Miller's. He ran through a list of locations between Miller's and their room above the saloon. Each option had its pluses and minuses. James would have to finalize scouting the perfect spot on his way to work in the morning. He drummed his fingers on the table as he thought. As he came back to the present moment, he thought Carson had said something to him.

"I'm sorry. Did you say something?"

"I said, back to square one." Carson looked annoyed at having to repeat himself.

"Back to square one." James echoed Carson. He scooped up his cards and fanned out his hand. "Aw, jeez." James studied his cards to find two threes, a ten, one jack and one queen. He clearly tipped the awful hand to Carson.

Carson giggled out loud, laughing so hard he let slip some loud gas. Both boys stared at each other in silence for a long moment. Then they both burst into raucous laughter.

CHAPTER 5

James swept the general store's porch. All morning he had tried to find a way to work out front but Mr. Miller had thwarted his plans several times. James had tried to redo the window displays so he could keep an eye on the street. Mr. Miller asked him to toss out the older produce instead. James attempted to wash the store windows but Mr. Miller had him dust the shelves.

While Mr. Miller ducked into the stockroom for a customer, James snatched up the broom and went outside to sweep. He wanted to finalize his plan for the annual apparition and he needed to see the various locations. Things hadn't worked out as he had hoped this morning. His intentions were to scout out safe viewing locations while he walked to work. However, James got waylaid by Miss Lark. The beautiful, young school teacher was struggling to carry a stack of supplies. James had offered to help her and she had accepted his offer happily. When they arrived at the schoolhouse, Miss Lark engaged James in a conversation about the legend of the ghost. The discussion had turned into an inquisition about his background and the town they used to live in before moving here. James was exasperated by how many questions the woman asked. Each time he answered one, another question soon followed. And he didn't want to rush things since Miss Lark was very pleasing to his eyes.

As he swept around the salt barrel, James spied the clock tower down the street. It was quarter to noon already. He noticed that the street had far less activity than usual for this hour of the day. Apparently, the townspeople took this legend very seriously and did their best to avoid an ill-timed stroll downtown.

James picked out two potential locations for his watch. One spot was really close to the action. It was a long horse trough in front of the post office. For some reason, the trough in that location was a few feet from the post office's porch. All the other troughs in town were situated right up against the porch boards. So this spot left some room for him to squat low enough behind the wood to protect himself. The problem with this location was that it was very close to the rumored area where the ghost would appear.

The second location was the alleyway between the haberdashery and the saloon. There were ample barrels and crates stacked along the edifice which would afford James a safe vantage. The downside of this location was that it was a bit behind the rumored area of the ghost and it was in direct sight of James' room. So, when his mother looked out the window to find out why James wasn't home yet like she expected, she would be able to see him crouched down in the alleyway.

Before he could decide on which spot to use, the door to the store opened as Mr. Miller walked a customer out. He immediately saw James and his bald head wrinkled up with anger.

"James. What on earth are you doing out here? I explicitly told you to dust the shelves, not sweep the porch." Mr. Miller rested his large hands on his hips to accentuate his disappointment.

"Yes, sir. I dusted the shelves and didn't want to stand around with nothing to do. So I figured I would clean out here a bit."

Mr. Miller glanced at the clock tower and quickly realized the time. "Oh my. I lost track of time. You were supposed to head home for lunch twenty minutes ago. Now give me that broom and run along. There is no more time to waste if you are to arrive home safely." He reached for the broom.

"Sorry, sir. I just have to finish one more thing before I go."

"Nonsense. You'll leave now and not waste another minute." Mr. Miller sternly pointed James toward home.

"I accidentally spilled some rice in the storeroom, sir. And I don't want mice to get into it. So I'll just be one minute to clean it up before I run home. I promise I'll be quick. And thorough." James played on Mr. Miller's obsession with cleanliness and order. He also knew the proprietor was deathly afraid of infestations of any kind, as it could ruin his business. Mr. Miller's expression went from anger to fear when he heard about mice.

"Very well. Make it quick. I'm going to lock up now so you'll have to leave through the back door. Now get going. I wouldn't be able to live with myself if something were to happen to you because you stayed too long at work."

James smiled and nodded his head. He scrambled through the door and ran between the shelves to the storeroom in the back. As he ran, he heard Mr. Miller close the door and secure the lock bar in place. James had lied to Mr. Miller to gain some more time. He hid for a few moments in the storeroom. The butterflies were going mad in his belly. In less than five minutes, he was going to see something that both excited him and frightened him at the same time. The last time he had felt like this, he was chasing his old friend Crouching Bear.

James ran through his options one last time. He decided to use the horse trough since his mother wouldn't be able to see him. Plus, he would have a front row seat to all the action. The flutter in his stomach shot some bile up his throat which he quickly swallowed down. The time had come to get into place. He opened the storeroom door and then closed it behind him. He saw Mr. Miller crouched down behind the register, his eyes just above the machine, staring out the front window.

"I'm off, Mr. Miller. See you after lunch." James shouted and waved to his boss, who he had clearly startled. James figured the man was scared of the ghost and his fast exit had only added to the old guy's fright. James dashed through the back door and slammed it shut as he ran past the buildings. He was in such a hurry that he never heard Mr. Miller wish him well on his way out.

"Godspeed, James." The man swallowed a huge lump in his throat and ducked back down behind the register.

CHAPTER 6

Mayor Samuels leaned back in the chair. His whiskers itched his cheeks and he liked being clean-shaven. Except for the goatee. The barber shop was busy this morning, probably because men wanted to get cleaned up before the ghost gunslinger showed up at noon. The Mayor was of the same mind but he wouldn't admit to that openly.

Clip Jones sharpened the razor along the strop as he spoke. Nobody in town really knew Clip's first name. He had introduced himself as Clip when he first opened shop and the name stuck on account of his profession. Clip was lean with strong arms. His jaw was square and accentuated by an extremely receding hairline.

"Y'all are gonna make me earn my money this morning. I haven't seen a line like this since the Gullickson funeral." He dragged the razor back and forth upon the leather.

Mr. Simpson scratched his stubble and joined the fray from the waiting area. "The missus wants me ta have a clean face 'afore the shootin' starts. An' she says I need ta have a clean face fer the undertaker lest I catch a bullet." He guffawed and the crowd of men joined in the nervous laughter.

Mayor Samuels spoke to the group, while he looked at them in the mirror. "Now I told you all that this fable is just malarkey. Nobody is going to be forced to meet with the undertaker today." Clip finished sharpening the razor and began applying shaving cream to the Mayor's cheeks and neck.

Simpson shot back at the Mayor. "Seems like you 'er thinkin' the sames as us, Samu'ls. Aintcha here ta git cleaned up fer the shootin' too?"

Clip Jones glared at Simpson, while he smoothed out the lather on the Mayor's face. "Now, mind your manners, Simpson. This is the Mayor of our town you are addressing here. And, if you get fresh, I'm going to have to ask you to leave."

Mayor Samuels raised a hand in Simpson's defense. "That's all right, Clip. The man has a right to speak his mind. God gives every man that right, regardless of which end the words are coming from." A round of applause and jeers flew up at the Mayor's retort. Simpson slapped his leg with his dusty hat and slumped down in his chair. When the noise abated, the Mayor got back on his soap box.

"I recognize that this story has everyone on edge. But it is just that. A story. Sometimes, when men believe so strongly in something, it has a tendency to come true." The men looked confused. "What I mean to say is that the ghost doesn't appear each year because the town believes in him. The ghost appears in our minds, and then the panic takes over and folks get all jumpy. And when folks get all jumpy, bullets fly and people get hurt."

Clip tugged the Mayor's ear back to get a closer shave along his sideburns. He had a tendency of screwing up his face while he worked, as if he were shaving himself. It was a crude display of life imitating art. "I buy that notion, Mr. Mayor. Really, I do. But we can't deny what happened several years ago when Sheriff Morgan got hit and Sammy Tucker took one in the keister. That actually happened."

"I'm not denying that it did happen, Clip. All I'm saying is that nobody knows for sure where those bullets came from. People think they saw shots coming from this ghostly image but lots of people had their guns pulled in sheer panic. It could have been shots from anybody's' gun." The Mayor rolled his head back and to the right so Clip could get under his jowls. A murmur of disagreement rumbled throughout the men awaiting their turn.

"Besides, descriptions of this ghost were inconsistent. Some saw a whitish shape, some saw a clear outline of a man, and still others couldn't describe it at all. Surely, if the ghost existed, at least two descriptions of it would have matched, don't you think?" The Mayor made some strong points but the men only shifted uneasily.

"I guess your explanation sounds as valid as any." Clip wiped the remaining streaks of shaving cream with a towel. "I still wouldn't tempt fate. I, for one, will be hidden in the shadows today at noon."

"There aren't any shadows at noon. Just to prove the legend isn't real, I will stroll across Main Street today and show the folks of this fine town that their fears are unfounded. This ghost story will come to an end today. I'll stake my life on it." The Mayor made sure to connect his gaze with each individual in the shop as he spoke. His final statement hovered like a dark cloud and most of the men averted their eyes, afraid the Mayor's defiance would drag them down too. They seemed superstitious. Simpson made the sign of the cross as protection.

Mayor Samuels stood up to check out his clean shave in the mirror. Clip Jones removed the chair cloth. As the Mayor leaned toward the mirror, he recognized the fear in his pupils. He did his best to make it look like he was inspecting the shave but it was just a ruse. Mayor Samuels looked deep into his frightened eyes, searching for something, anything he could hang his hat on to convince himself not to follow through on his promise. His love for the town and his egotistical desire to remain a steadfast leader of the town had backed him into this corner. He feared for his life because deep down in his gut, he knew the gunslinger was real. And he had sentenced himself to death.

The Mayor reached into his pocket for a coin. His nervous fingers fumbled for a moment in his trousers. He removed the coin and handed it to Clip Jones.

"A fine job, Clip. A fine job."

"Thank you, Mayor. But I couldn't accept your payment today. This one is on the house."

The Mayor tilted his head in surprise. "Are you saying my money is no good?"

"Not at all, Mr. Mayor." Clip searched for the right words. "It's just that I would like to show my appreciation for your bravery today in the face of our horrifying visitor." Clip looked at the men gathered in the waiting area. The men did anything but look at the barber or the Mayor. Some studied their boots while others brushed off their hats or cleaned their dirty fingernails.

"Bravery has nothing to do with it. It's confidence that everything will work out just fine. Now you keep that money because you earned it. And I won't hear another word about it."

Clip extended his hand and the Mayor shook it. As the Mayor turned to leave the barber shop, he couldn't help but notice the silence. Not one man looked at him as he strode towards the door.

CHAPTER 7

Carson played solitaire at the table. He found peace in a deck of cards. Something about the smoothed edges and the square stack in his small hands felt good. Of course, he preferred to play card games with someone else. He loved to win games and playing alone didn't produce the same happiness he felt when he would beat the pants off James.

His mind clicked through the numbers and suits as he worked out the combinations before him. Sarah was stirring a pot of lentil soup on the cast iron stove. She lifted the wooden spoon to her lips and blew on it before tasting it. Carson watched her as his belly growled and his mouth flooded with saliva.

Sarah looked at the little clock next to the bed and saw that it was nearly noon. "Where is that boy? He should have been here by now."

Carson giggled. He knew why James wasn't home yet.

"What's so funny, Carson?"

He sat up and stopped laughing. "Um, nothing."

"Then why did you just laugh?"

"I don't know."

"You don't know?" Sarah approached the table. She lowered her eyes on Carson to pressure him into giving up the goods. "Something had to have made you laugh. Is it me?"

Carson couldn't help himself. He giggled again.

"Then what is it you find so funny?"

"James."

Sarah's eyebrows knit together. Her crystal-blue eyes searched Carson's face. "What about James?"

"He's hiding." Carson giggled.

"He's hiding what?"

"He's hiding for the ghost."

Sarah panicked. "He's what? What do you mean he's hiding for the ghost?" She glanced around the room as if James might jump out from under the bed or from behind the changing panel.

Carson realized, by her reaction, that he had done something bad. His face sunk and the laughter died away. He wasn't supposed to say anything. James swore him not tell his mother the plan for watching the ghost. James was supposed to see the ghost and then come home and tell his mother that he got caught up at work. And then he had decided to stay in the store for safety. Carson felt warm tears fill his eyes. He wasn't supposed to tell and now James would never trust him again.

Sarah stepped forward and grabbed Carson by the shoulders. She implored him to provide more information. "Where is he? Where is James hiding? Is he in this building?" The questions flew out of her mouth.

Carson couldn't respond. His lips trembled with disappointment that he couldn't do the one thing James had asked of him. He didn't understand how it came out of him so easily. Carson pointed a finger at the window that looked over the street above the saloon.

Sarah let go of Carson and ran to the window. She raised it higher so she could poke her head out to see. Her eyes searched the street, both up and down. There didn't appear to be any pedestrians or movement outside. A quiet hush filled the air.

Carson pushed his chair back and hurried to the window too. He didn't want to miss the ghost. He squeezed under Sarah's arm to lean over the window sill. Carson rubbed the lingering tears from his eyes as his betrayal washed away with the excitement of the coming apparition. He really wanted to help James fight the ghost but he knew he wouldn't be able to escape James' mother.

Sarah backed away from the window and tugged Carson's arm. "You need to stay away from the window. What if this...this thing is real and a bullet flies up here. I don't want you to get hurt."

"I won't get hurt." Carson responded innocently.

"Promise me you will not go near the window. I need to know that you are safe. I have to go find James before he gets hurt. So promise me you will not go near the window." Sarah repeated herself as her eyes begged Carson to comply.

Carson looked down at the floor then back into Sarah's eyes. "I promise." He said the words but he had no intention of doing as she asked.

"Good. I love you." She kissed his forehead and turned to leave. "I'll be back shortly with James. Remember, stay away from that window." She pointed at the glass again. Just then the clock tower chimed the first of twelve bells. It was noon. And time had run out for the town.

Sarah gasped when she heard the first chime. She charged through the door and slammed it behind her. Carson heard her footsteps run down the hall to the staircase. He turned on his heels and ran back to the window. Carson stuck his head out and leaned as far over the sill as he could without falling down to the street. He wanted to make sure he didn't miss a thing.

Carson wondered where James was hiding. His eyes searched for James as another bell chimed. Carson hoped James didn't fight the ghost today because he wanted to be part of the battle too. James told him he was only going to watch today so he could come up with a better plan to fight the ghost next year. But Carson wasn't sure if he believed James. He had no reason to distrust his best friend. Something in James' eyes had shown Carson maybe James said things just to protect him. He didn't think James meant any harm towards him. Yet, he had a suspicion James would rather lie to him than get him mixed up in something he couldn't handle.

Carson smiled as another bell chimed. He was confident he could do anything James could do. They were a team. They both shared the same dreams of riding out of town and saving people from crooked men. James wanted to be like his daddy. Carson wanted to be someone different. He didn't understand what that meant but he knew deep inside he wanted to be his own type of hero. He knew he was different from other folks. More than a few people had called him names and made him feel less than a person. Which is why Carson aspired to be bigger than life. He would show everyone. Someday, he would be a hero. And James would be by his side.

Carson shifted his hands to change his view. His eyes scanned Main Street, looking for the ghost and his best friend in the whole world.

CHAPTER 8

Time was slipping by quickly. Folks in town had been edgy and in a hurry all morning. The foreboding of the annual ghostly visit had people nervous and moving quickly. People wanted to make sure they got important packages mailed or picked up their daily groceries. The whole town tried to squeeze an entire day into three or four hours. Because nobody wanted to be out and about when the gunslinger arrived.

Most folks ran their errands in silence, preferring not to tempt fate by acknowledging the abhorrent day. Heads down and feet moving with expedient purpose. While others worried with neighbors or co-workers about the potential disruption. Spoken or not, the mood infected everyone on some level.

The hardware store and lumber yard chose to keep their doors closed today. A sign in front of the lumber yard read, "Closed until further notice." The further notice would probably be the undertaker's request for wood to construct a coffin, or two. The haberdashery and the post office posted signs for an "extended" lunch break. One stated it would re-open at 2 p.m., while the other was 3 p.m.

The establishments that remained open were the saloon, the apothecary, Doc Stinson's office, Clip's Barber Shop and Miller's General Store. Of course, if anybody had inquired with each proprietor about their plans for the noon hour, to a man, they would admit they planned to lock the doors and keep a vigilant eye upon Main Street.

The clock tower reached into the blue sky, brick red juxtaposed against the white cumulus clouds that drifted by. Its white face smiled down over Main Street, as its blackened hands spun upon their axes. The hour hand was firmly on twelve. While the minute hand moved toward the same mark. Within minutes, both hands would point to heaven and signal the noon hour.

A man on his horse glanced at the tower and tugged the reins to leave the center of town. A woman walked quickly, while holding her hooped skirt up off the dirty street. She spied the time and increased her pace towards the apothecary. Several others hurried along on their way into buildings, away from the momentary visitation.

Above Main Street, windows were sliding down and latches were being switched into place. A balcony door was secured with a squeaky turn of the lock. Blinds were being drawn, shades were pulled down and curtains were draped over windows. People still believed that if they couldn't see the evil spirit, then the evil spirit must not be able to see them. It was a childish notion, but one that couldn't be avoided regardless of age.

Silence settled over the town. The time had arrived. Everyone wondered to themselves. Would they see the gunslinger today?

CHAPTER 9

James made his way through the debris that had accumulated behind the buildings. Old wagons with missing wheels or barrels with holes littered the landscape. Excess lumber and iron parts teetered atop some of the refuse.

As James worked his way between the garbage, he envisioned the gunslinger's appearance. In his mind's eye, the gunslinger would start to glow out of thin air, forming a shape that resembled a man. The man would be pudgy with a messy mustache and a tall hat. His ghostly spurs would clink and a wailing moan would escape the man's dead lips. James could almost smell the rotting flesh of the corpse as it shot its way down Main Street.

His breathing grew cumbersome from his efforts to hurry through the junk. His heart hammered in his chest. The feeling of the adrenaline pumping through his veins brought back bittersweet memories of Iowa.

James rounded the end of the building and sprinted, up the alley, towards the center of town. A plume of dust followed his feet. He noticed a sheen of sweat forming along his brow, from the mid-day heat and the exertion. As he reached the end of the alley, James paused to see that the town looked abandoned. Not a soul stirred. No horses tied to railings. No dogs wandering the porches for scraps of food. Just a silent, barren town. James thought to himself that this must be what a true ghost town feels like. Empty and creepy.

He covered the remaining twenty yards to the horse trough in front of the post office. James dove along the dirt and slid in behind the wood structure. An odor of sweat mixed with horse dung surrounded the trough. James slowly raised his eyes above the top of the wood to peer across the street. He noticed a few faces peeking around curtains or tucked in the cracks of doorways. The town felt empty but it was full of fearful eyes.

James looked up at the clock tower and the minute hand was a shade to the left of the twelve. Only seconds remained before the much anticipated specter visited. The butterflies had stopped fluttering in his belly, as the bile replaced them. Fear had stepped in where excitement once stood. His ears were ringing due to the overwhelming silence. Not even the wind, which was ever present in Kansas, dared to make a sound.

He started to second guess his ability to take on the spirit on behalf of the town. What made him think he was so special that he could rid the town of a dark, otherworldly force? What if he was just lucky back in Iowa? And, even if it was skill, hadn't he needed the help of the medicine man and his friend George? Neither of which would be here to help this time. All his confidence and dreams of glory died away. He felt his hands shaking and the muscles in his thighs twitched with dread. What had he gotten himself into? It was bad enough he had pretended he could take on an evil ghost, but he actually set himself right in its path by coming outside. He felt so foolish.

The clock tower chimed loudly. The sound was deafening in the empty street. James jumped at the noise before his mind told his body that it was the clock and not a pistol. His head turtled back down behind the trough. Then he raised his eyes once more to see what might happen. Thoughts returned to his mother and Carson. He knew his mother would be worried sick about him not coming home on time, as she had expected. He figured that worry would turn to anger once he got home later. Or if he got home. Alive.

He chastised himself quietly for the risk he was taking with Carson. He had promised to look out for the boy and help raise him like a brother. Instead, he was risking his life for a fantasy. What if he died out here? Who would protect Carson? Would his mother be able to handle that responsibility plus run the brothel all by herself? James was sure she could handle anything, but hadn't she been burdened enough in life? She had raised him in a whorehouse on next to nothing and now, because of his mistakes, she had gotten dragged into caring for Carson too. She deserved better than this. James' heart swelled with sorrow for how hard his mother's life had been.

Another chime from the clock tower shook James out of his reverie. He glanced up and down Main Street but nothing had appeared. Yet.

James focused on his nervousness now that he was back in the moment. The shaking and twitching in his extremities belied his apprehension. Part of him wished Carson were by his side. Whenever James was around Carson, he felt more sure of himself. He didn't know if it was because Carson was slow, which made him feel brighter. Or the fact that he was so dedicated to looking out for the boy, it didn't leave him much time to think about his own self-doubts. He whispered to himself that it was most likely the second reason.

A third chime rang from the clock tower. James lowered his head and squeezed his eyes shut. He said a quick prayer and then quietly asked the Lord to protect his mother and Carson. Even in this dangerous moment, he was more concerned with their welfare than his own. The thought made him question his sanity, as he was the one in the direct line of fire. Literally and figuratively.

James glanced over the trough again. He heard the sound of a door clicking shut across the street. His eyes followed the sound and he couldn't believe what he saw. The Mayor had exited Clip's Barber Shop. The portly man stood defiantly on the porch outside the shop. James could see a clump of faces pressed up against the window from inside the barber shop. The expressions on the men's faces were of terror.

The clock tower chimed again.

Mayor Samuels lit a cigarette and shook out the match stick. He flung it into the street and puffed a huge cloud of smoke. The Mayor looked left and then right, up each end of Main Street.

The clock tower chimed.

The Mayor took several hesitant steps forward, stepping off the porch and onto the street. James fought the urge to scream to the Mayor to duck or hide. Surely the man knew what time it was. And hadn't James heard that the Mayor insisted that the legend of the ghost gunslinger was a fairytale? Even so, why would he risk his life to prove it?

Another chime of the clock tower.

James was beside himself. The desire for self-preservation battled with his instincts for helping others. He wondered if this was his moment for heroism, saving the Mayor from the gunslinger, rather than defeating the ghost.

DONG.

James whispered a quick prayer for the Mayor and watched the street from behind the trough.

CHAPTER 10

Mayor Samuels reached for the door knob with a shaky hand. He hoped nobody had witnessed his obvious fear. He felt the eyes on his back; the same eyes that had avoided his as he approached the door. The moment had arrived and there was no turning back now.

He turned the knob and stepped out onto the porch. The clock tower bell had already chimed. It sounded off again.

His eyes scanned the street. Nothing stirred. His memory couldn't recall any time in which this street was not bustling with traffic. Even when they had first built this town, Main Street was a constant scene of noise and chaos. Men shouting and cussing. Horses trotting. Wagons toting goods and supplies. The Mayor knew it got like this each year when the gunslinger arrived, but only since the Sheriff and Tucker had gotten shot. And the Mayor hadn't seen those times since he was hiding in his office like a coward, feigning disdain and indifference for the town's belief in the legend.

The clock tower rang.

He opened his coat and removed a cigarette from his pocket. Again, his hand shook as it retrieved his smoke. The Mayor struck a match against the support beam and fired his cigarette. The smoke scratched his throat but soothed his nerves. He tossed the match stick into the dirt.

Another chime.

The Mayor took a long drag on the cigarette. He held the smoke deep in his lungs for several seconds before exhaling a huge cloud of smoke into the still air. He noticed that it was probably the first time in his life that there wasn't even the slightest breeze in Kansas. He wondered if even the wind was smart enough to hide from the monstrous spirit.

DONG.

The eyes from the men in the barber shop behind him filled his back with needles. The sense of their stares overwhelmed him. It made him realize that there was so much that man still didn't understand about the world. All the unseen. Like sensations and ghosts. He asked himself what else he didn't know but should.

His life began to kaleidoscope before his eyes. Working on his grand pappy's farm. The time he broke his leg when he fell out of a tree. His fight with his daddy over control of the farm. Leaving home to find his true calling in life, but mostly to escape his daddy's iron fist. The newspaper proclaiming the new settlement in Wichita. The road to town, filled with danger from the Indians, the beasts and, of course, unscrupulous settlers. And then the day he had arrived here. The sounds and smells. So many people in one spot. The excitement of a fresh start. The women. Definitely the women. Like nothing he had ever known before.

Another chime.

A tear streaked down his cheek and he realized he had been crying as he recalled the life that led up to this moment. He snorted his runny nose and took a few steps forward. As he stepped off the porch onto the dirt street, his knees buckled a bit. He took the cigarette away from his mouth. The paper had stuck to his dried lips.

The Mayor extended his arms like Jesus on the cross and strode into the street. He spun in a slow circle and addressed the peering eyes. "Ain't nothing to fear." He circled. "Just a man. Standing. In the street."

The clock tower sounded.

He tried to remember how many times the clock had rung. But he realized he had lost count. He thought it didn't really matter much at this point.

As he turned, he saw the faces. People stared at him from windows and behind curtains. Everyone wore the same expression. Their eyes wide to absorb everything. Their jaws hung open as they held their breath in wait.

"No such thing as the gunslinger." His voice cracked. He hoped it didn't sound as bad to the townspeople as it did within his own ears.

The clock tower chimed.

"I told you all it was hogwash. An old wive's tale. A campfire story to scare folks."

The Mayor was feeling a bit more confident. With each chime and no appearance yet of the gunslinger, Mayor Samuels began to think he might be vindicated. His own legend for being the man who built this town and kept it running safely would expand. Generations to come would remember him for his achievements, but most of all, for conquering the haunted gunslinger. Adding the supernatural to his resume would only further ingrain him in the spirit of the town. Maybe they would name a building after him. Or maybe rename the town. Samuelstown has a nice ring to it. There would be a monument. No. A statue. Yeah, definitely a statue.

DONG.

He took one more drag of the cigarette and then flung the butt into the center of Main Street. The smoke billowed through his nostrils as he searched the windows for a response. The Mayor chuckled out loud. His confidence had come back as he envisioned a glorious victory. Perhaps the annual visitation was finished. But the folks of the town would think it was because of his willingness to stand up to it. To face down the evil and live life unopposed. He had always had a flair for the dramatic. He figured it was time to goose the act to embellish his legend.

The clock tower rang.

"I ain't afraid of you, gunslinger. I don't believe in your power or your presence." Mayor Samuels placed his hands on his hips in a display of impatience. "You're just a washed up fairy tale. Unimportant." He wanted to raise the bar a little. Give something to the bible-thumpers. "The Lord has damned you to eternal hell. To burn with Satan and his followers."

Another chime sounded.

The gap between bells extended as the Mayor realized the clock was finished. Twelve chimes had sounded. He turned and looked behind him. There was nothing. He faced forward and still there was no ghost.

The Mayor squinted in the sunlight as a faint breeze picked up some dust. He thought to himself that it was over. The wind was back. The noon time had struck. And there was no sign of the gunslinger.

He had to put an exclamation point on the scene. Something that would look good in the newspaper headlines in bold print. A quote to be remembered in history books and repeated around dinner tables.

"I am Mayor Thomas Samuels. I don't fear you. Take your best shot right now or forever burn in hell." He stretched his arms outward once again like he was nailed to a cross. A vision of vulnerability sprinkled with defiance.

CHAPTER 11

As the Mayor stood in the middle of town, a disturbance emanated from the end of Main Street. It sounded like a static, crackling noise. The sound was faint, but discernible. Small flashes of light popped several times and then a shape took form within the flashes. The shape was hazy at first and then filled slowly with color. This form was more solid than the ghost which had appeared in the past. It was sheer at first but then became opaque. It was the gunslinger.

The gunslinger was tall and lean. He had short gray hair and a coal black mustache which was neatly trimmed. His eyes were blacker than night. The gunslinger wore a long, leather duster over his black pants and ruby-colored shirt. The hat on his head was also black. The top was short and flat.

Mayor Samuel's face drooped. His arms were frozen in the outstretched position. His eyes opened wide with horror. The Mayor's mouth opened as if he wanted to say something but no words came forth. His lips just trembled.

James fought his bowels from loosening. He rubbed his eyes as if he had just awoken from a long nap, not believing the apparition before him. He swallowed hard and felt his breath seize in his chest.

The gunslinger took two steps forward in the direction of the Mayor. The spurs clinked with each boot touching down. He swung his duster back with both arms, revealing two gun belts overlapping each other. A shiny six shooter hung on each hip, looking out of place among the dirty clothing. His eyes narrowed so that wrinkled laugh lines spread outward toward his sideburns.

"Wha...wha...wha..." The Mayor stammered to speak but gibberish is all that came out. He wet himself as he stood before the ghost.

The gunslinger drew both pistols in less than a second and spun the weapons around his fingers. The guns came to a rest in his palms and he fired a shot from each. Both rounds skittered on either side of the Mayor. They were warning shots.

"Nobody makes fun of me or questions my existence." The gunslinger spoke with a raspy voice that sounded like sand swirled around in his throat.

The Mayor dropped to his knees, arms still outstretched. The legs could no longer support the heavy body as all blood rushed to his brain in a last ditch effort for survival.

The gunslinger squeezed off two more rounds. One struck the Mayor squarely in the chest. Blood splattered through his white shirt. The second round went right between the Mayor's eyes. He was dead before his body slumped to the dirt.

James tucked his head down with each shot. His breathing had returned, hard and sporadic. He couldn't believe what he was seeing. Not only was he witness to a ghost, which was beyond comprehension, but he was also witness to the death of the town's popular mayor. He heard somebody screaming "No" in a loud voice. James peered carefully over the trough to see Sheriff Axl Morgan sprinting up the street towards the Mayor's body.

The gunslinger fired several more shots. The ghost laughed a creaky, wicked laugh, which immediately sent chills down James' spine. Each shot was dodged by the sheriff as he kept coming. Sheriff Morgan reached the Mayor's body and crouched down next to it. He pulled his pistol from the holster and fired several shots of his own at the gunslinger. Two shots went wide but the third struck the gunslinger in the belly. There was just one problem. The bullet passed through the gunslinger's midsection as if he wasn't even there.

Sheriff Morgan realized the shot had no effect so he dropped the pistol in the dirt and picked up the Mayor under his arms. As he began to drag the corpse back down the street, two more shots struck the Mayor's chest, spraying blood onto the front of the sheriff's clothes. He dropped down to the dirt, using the Mayor's body as a shield.

James couldn't sit on the sidelines any longer. He sprang up and leaped over the horse trough. His first thought was to run to the Sheriff to help him escape. But as quickly as he thought this, James decided it was no use. The gunslinger would just continue to take free shots at the men. So his instinct snapped him into action. James charged the gunslinger at a full sprint.

The gunslinger heard James coming his way and swung on his heels to face the threat. He pulled the triggers and two more shots whistled past James. One scratched James' cheek with a searing heat. The other narrowly missed his head as he ducked while running. The gunslinger aimed again and squeezed the triggers. But both pistols were empty. The guns clicked over and over as the ghost kept pulling the triggers.

James zigged and zagged as he ran toward the apparition to avoid the bullets. His body kept the pattern even though the hammers clicked on empty chambers. James swallowed a lump and felt a surge of adrenaline run through his veins. Now he had a chance to stop the gunslinger before he could reload. He had no idea how that would happen but he was determined to give it his all.

The gunslinger spun his pistols around his fingers again and then re-holstered them. He croaked the same evil laughter as he stared right through James with his black eyes. "I'll be back for you." The ghost spoke without moving his lips, yet James heard the voice inside his head. "James." The gunslinger knowing his name stopped James dead in his tracks. He was confused that a ghost could know who he was when he had never seen it before. The chills shot from his spine, through his limbs, as he understood the evil that must exist for such a power to be possible.

With a fading cackle, the gunslinger disappeared amid light flashes and more sizzling sounds. In a matter of seconds, the gunslinger was gone and the street had returned to an eerie silence.

James turned and saw the sheriff crawling out from under the Mayor's bloodied body. He stood and dusted himself off as James neared. On each side of the street, doors were opening and windows were sliding up. All the eyes that hid in safety turned into full faces and folks slowly wandered into the street to inspect the carnage. Nobody spoke a word, as everyone was in shock.

James looked down at the Mayor's face. The hole between his eyes trickled blood, which pooled in the open eyelids. The wounds in his chest left gaping holes that bubbled with the last remnants of oxygen escaping the lungs. He stood in disbelief at how fast everything had happened. So many emotions had filtered through the last five minutes or so. He raised his head and looked at Sheriff Axl Morgan.

The Sheriff's eyes stared back at James, as the town crowded in to get a closer look.

CHAPTER 12

James didn't like jail. He felt the walls close in around him. The cell was very small. He estimated it to be about four feet by eight feet in size. Just wide enough for a dusty cot. And deep enough to give him nearly a foot of space to stand before the cot. He leaned against the iron bars and watched the mob outside.

Sheriff Morgan had dragged James by the collar the whole way to the cell. He had shoved James inside and then slammed the bars shut. Then he locked the office, leaving James behind. At first, James was angry. He didn't understand why he was in trouble for trying to help defeat the gunslinger. James swore he would give Sheriff Morgan a good piece of his mind when the lawman returned. But, as time passed, James' anger deflated. Plus, he felt safer in the jail cell, considering the crowd that had accumulated outside.

James tried to make out what the mob was saying. All he could pick up were muffled arguments peppered with shouted cuss words. It was clear the townspeople were upset, but James didn't know if the anger was directed at him or the sheriff or even the gunslinger.

He plopped down on the cot and chewed a hang nail on his middle finger. James wondered how upset his mother was. He knew he was in for it whenever she got near him next. He deserved to be in trouble with her for lying about his plans. But not for doing what he could to help the people in town. James felt like a grown man these days. Especially after what had happened in their last town. And more so now that he had a paying job to support the family. He was nearly eighteen, and he was old enough to make his own decisions.

His mind skipped to Carson, as he gently rubbed the superficial wound on his cheek. James hoped Carson knew he was okay. The thought of the little guy worrying about him made James uncomfortable. The poor kid had been through enough hard times in recent memory. The last thing James wanted was to add to Carson's nightmares.

James replayed the shootout in his mind. The ghost had been far more realistic than he had imagined. If he didn't know any better, James would have sworn that the gunslinger was a living, breathing person. Except for those eyes. His eyes had been blacker than coal. And cavernous. It was like you could look straight through a long, dark tunnel to hell in those eyes.

But how could something ethereal become so real? And what about the bullets? How does an apparition get their hands on bullets? Did it use real bullets? Or were they ghostly slugs conjured up from the bottom of hell? James struggled with fitting the pieces together. Every theory he came up with just led to more questions. Questions he had no answers to. He needed to find out who the gunslinger was. If he could learn the ghost's true identity, he could figure out what causes the annual visit.

James got restless again. He stood and grasped the iron bars to the cell. He tried to shake the iron bars with all his strength but they didn't budge. He didn't really think they would but the nervous energy was searching for an outlet.

Suddenly, the shouting outside grew louder. James heard a set of keys jingle and then the tumblers in the lock clicked. The door to the Sheriff's office opened. The mob's cries were deafening without the damper of a locked door. Sheriff Morgan stepped into the office and forced the door closed against a throng of angry townspeople. He quickly locked the door from the inside.

"What's going on out there? And why did you lock me up, Sheriff? I haven't done anything wrong?"

Sheriff Morgan stared at James beneath the brim of his hat. His fingers toiled with the ring of keys in his hand. He tossed the keys on his desk and approached the jail cell.

"The protection is for you, not the folks outside."

James blinked with confusion. "Huh?"

The Sheriff turned and walked to his desk. He removed his hat and placed it upon the desk. Then he folded his arms and leaned against the far wall. "Those folks want to kill you, James."

"Me? What for?"

"Seems the Mayor's blood is on your hands. At least according to them."

"But how? Surely they all witnessed me charge the gunslinger. Besides, I didn't even have a gun so how could I have shot the Mayor?"

"Everyone knows you didn't pull the trigger. But your involvement in the incident and the fact that you are new in town has folks spooked."

James was incredulous. He was at a loss for words.

"You see, James. People in this here town have a certain…way about them. They work hard. They drink hard. And they are God-fearing. These people have learned to avoid the gunslinger's antics. Until today."

"But what does that have to do with me?"

"Until today," the Sheriff continued, "nobody got killed. Now you come to town and run up on the gunslinger. And the most revered man in town history is dead. Don't you think that seems odd?"

James listened with frustration. But this accusation pushed his temper over the top. "Now you listen, Sheriff. The Mayor walked into the street on his own. He taunted the gunslinger himself. And I'm awful sorry that he is dead. But I am not going to stand here and accept blame for something I didn't do."

"No, you listen, James." The Sheriff got close to the iron bars. His face was just inches from James. "It doesn't matter what you did or didn't do. And it doesn't matter what you or I think you did or didn't do. It matters what they all think." He pointed behind himself at the shouting crowd outside.

"So you believe me?"

"Course I do, son. I saw it with my own dang eyes."

"Then…why am I still locked up in here?"

"Well, until I can figure out what to do, that's the only place where those folks can't rip you to shreds." The Sheriff went back to his desk and sat down. James watched the Sheriff, while his mind scrambled for ways to get out of this mess. James had never imagined that being a hero would be so troublesome. He thought to himself how the newspapers and books never mentioned these types of issues when they sensationalized the stories. For the first time in his life, James wondered how much truth was included in all the tales he read.

CHAPTER 13

The pounding on the window startled Sheriff Morgan out of his reverie. He had fallen trance-like into deep thought about what to do with James. The loud rapping on the glass shook him back to the present moment. Sheriff Morgan recognized the woman as Sarah Johnson, the new madam of the brothel. He nodded to her and strode to the door of his office. The Sheriff did his best to unlock the door without allowing a horde of angry residents in. He shoved a portly fellow who blocked the way so Sarah could squeeze inside.

Before the Sheriff could slam the door shut, another person ducked under his arm. He quickly barred the door and spun to address the uninvited guest.

"Uh, Miss Lark? What in hell do you think you are doing? And pardon my language, ma'am." Sheriff Morgan tipped the brim of his hat at the young school teacher as a sign of respect.

The young woman tried to catch her breath after pushing her way through the angry crowd in order to gain access. She unsuccessfully tidied the bun in her hair and straightened her dress sleeves. Then she cleared her throat.

"I wanted to check on James, Sheriff. He is being treated unfairly by the town and I am here to stand up for the young man."

Sarah pushed Sheriff Morgan aside and stepped into Miss Lark. "Who are you? And what business is it of yours that James is here?" Sarah's crystal-blue eyes narrowed with mistrust.

Miss Lark extended her hand to Sarah. "I am Miss Lark. Eleanor Lark. I'm the school teacher here in town. Pleased to meet you."

Sarah pushed Miss Lark's hand aside. Sheriff Morgan intervened before the inside of his office reflected the chaos that existed on the outside.

"Okay, okay. Let's settle down here." He removed his hat and tossed it on the desk. "Now, what makes you think James needs speaking for?"

"Well, clearly, Sheriff, you have locked up this poor boy and turned the town against him. But I know James. And James would never have caused the Mayor's demise like everyone is talking about."

"Can I say something?" James tried to interject.

"No." The three voices shouted in unison. They looked at each other and James just huffed and sat down on the cot in the cell.

"How do you know James? We're new in town and I don't see how you would have had time to get to know my son?" Sarah's eyes shot back toward James, who avoided her glare.

"James helped me with my books this morning. We got to speaking and he purported to be a fine young man." Miss Lark's cheeks blushed at her admission of acquaintance.

"I don't know what purported means but if you laid a finger on that…" Sarah revealed her over-protective nature before the Sheriff once again intervened.

"Sarah, please. Take a seat." Sarah stared at the Sheriff with a look of disobedience so he took it up a notch. "Sit. Now." He pointed at his desk chair. Sarah stared at Miss Lark as she walked around the edge of the desk to seat herself.

"I really have something to say." James tried again.

"Oh, you'll say nothing, Mister. Just you wait until I get you home." Sarah shoved her finger in James' direction. James rolled his eyes and sat back down.

Sheriff Morgan smirked at the exchange in his office. The circumstances were serious but he seemed to find it a bit entertaining as well. Things had been slow in town, which is always a good thing for a sheriff. But this lively tat-on-tat was funny, he thought.

"Okay. So here we are. James is in trouble. The town wants to lynch him. And we need to figure out how to get him out of this."

Sarah looked at Sheriff Morgan. "You mean, you don't think he is guilty?"

"Aw, hell no." Sheriff Morgan replied and then realized he had cussed again. "Pardon me; I saw the events unfold before my own eyes. I know James had nothing to do with the Mayor dying. I just locked him up to protect him from them." He tossed his thumb over his shoulder toward the crowd.

Sarah visibly softened. "Oh. That's a relief. Thank you, Sheriff."

"Don't thank me yet, Miss Johnson. James is still in hot water."

"Well what if we told the proper story to the folks? They would have to believe us if they listened." Miss Lark stole a glance at James and blushed when their eyes met.

The Sheriff shook his head. "Most everyone saw what happened. They know James didn't pull the trigger. But he being new in these parts and the fact that he attempted to intervene has folks stirred up." He looked at the women and then continued. "Folks in this here town are superstitious. They feel James' actions may be linked to what occurred on a more sinister level." He rested his hands on his holster.

"They think James put a curse on the town?" Miss Lark looked shocked.

"Not a curse. But…maybe a jinx. I don't know what to call it. But them folks think James is tied to the Mayor's death."

"So what can we do to convince them otherwise?" Sarah raised her eyebrows in hopes of finding a solution.

"Uh, I can help my own cause here." James stood again and grasped the iron bars. This time the three faces turned toward him without quieting him. James felt relieved that he finally had a chance to speak. "All I was trying to do was defeat the gunslinger. I want a chance to take him down. And I'll tell these good folks what I aim to do."

Sarah shot James a look like she wanted him to refrain from revealing his previous encounter with Crouching Bear. The last thing she wanted was for people to know who James was and what he had done in the past. Things had gone so well up to this point in their new life and she didn't want to jeopardize their good fortune.

"Why would they want to listen to you, James?" Sheriff Morgan approached the iron bars.

"Because they want the gunslinger gone. And I'm going to fight for them."

"They'll tear you apart, James. Ain't nothing one man can do against an angry mob."

"But I'm not alone. I have you." James held his gaze with the Sheriff.

Sheriff Morgan tried to read James. Then he looked at Miss Lark who beamed. Sarah placed her head in her hands and sighed.

CHAPTER 14

"So that's it then? We're supposed to take yer word for it and let this boy loose to fight a ghost?" Mr. Black folded his arms. "Ain't he done enough damage around here?"

The crowd that gathered in the saloon rumbled as folks debated the Sheriff's plan. James still felt the butterflies in his gut. The town meeting had started over two hours ago and the crowd was still undecided. James looked at Sheriff Morgan who continued to search the room for an agreeable face.

"I'm not a boy. I'm almost eighteen." James shouted over the din. The room erupted in laughter at James characterizing himself as a man. Carson's face was scrunched at the people in the saloon. He walked up to Mr. Black and tugged on his vest.

"Hey, Mister. James is a hero. And he can fighted any bad guy in the whole world. Ain't that right, James?"

James grinned at his little buddy. He enjoyed Carson's newfound brashness. James wondered if Carson was growing up and coming out of his shell or just mad at Mr. Black for speaking ill of his friend.

Mr. Black shoved Carson away. "Am I supposed to take yer word for it, retart?" He bellowed laughter and the room followed suit.

"What did you say to him?" James hurried to Mr. Black's spot and stood right before him. The laughter wound down as the townspeople prepared themselves for the beating they all felt James deserved.

Mr. Black returned James' glare. "Whoa now, boy. You might find yerself barking up the wrong tree. I suggest you take a step back 'afore I show you what a real man is like." He moved his chaw from one cheek to the other. "And take that retarded mongrel with you."

The crowd mumbled with anticipation. James never took his eyes off Mr. Black.

Sheriff Morgan stepped up. "Listen, Black. You better square yourself away or you'll spend the night locked up."

Without looking away from James, Mr. Black snorted. "Yer gonna need a lot of deputies, Sheriff, if you think yer gonna take me in." Several of the men behind Mr. Black nodded that they were with him in times of trouble.

"Apologize to Carson."

"What?"

"Apologize to Carson, right now." James fumed through his nostrils.

"Or what?"

James head butted Mr. Black to the sound of cartilage crunching. Mr. Black dropped to his knees with blood gushing from the smashed appendage. His posse stepped forward but Sheriff Morgan pulled his pistol and cocked the hammer. The sound of the six-shooter stopped everyone in their tracks.

James leaned down to Mr. Black and whispered in his ear. "A real man knows when he is wrong. And when to apologize." Then he kicked his boot with all his might into Mr. Black's crotch. The man dropped to the floor and cried out in pain. His posse scooped him up and dragged Mr. Black out the door.

Suddenly, the room was listening to James with rapt attention. "I'm sorry for having to do that in front of y'all. But nobody treats my fr…" James caught himself, "my brother like that. Anybody that does wrong to Carson will answer to me."

Sheriff Morgan rested his hand on James' shoulder to let him know everything was settled now. "That's it, folks. You heard the plan. James is going to help us conquer this apparition. And we're going to help him.

Any way we can. If I find out that anybody gets in his way, then they will spend some time at my place in close quarters. Understood?"

The crowd shuffled restlessly. Some heads nodded understanding while others chose to just stare ahead to avoid agreeing, or being seen disagreeing. Sheriff Morgan took his time glancing from face to face.

"Best be on your way then. Have a good night."

The saloon thinned out as most folks returned to their homes. A few groups of patrons sidled up to the bar or grabbed seats at tables in the back. Sarah approached the Sheriff and James with her arm around Carson's shoulder.

"You got 'em good, James." Carson smiled up to James. James tousled Carson's hair.

"Do me a favor, James. Next time, keep the fighting to a minimum, huh?" Sheriff Morgan's sarcastic tone showed his displeasure.

James nodded. "Sorry. But I won't allow anybody to mess with Carson."

Carson rocked back and forth with a wide smile that suggested the Sheriff should put something in a pipe and smoke it. The Sheriff grimaced.

"So what happens next?" Sarah addressed the Sheriff. He tilted his hat back on his head and toed some dirt on the wood floor.

"I guess we need to finalize the plan and prepare James for a showdown."

"Already prepared." James retrieved the pistol from the back of his belt loop. He held it up and spun the cylinder which earned a giggle from Carson.

Sheriff Morgan lowered James' hand. "That piece is useless against the gunslinger. My shot went clear through it with no damage. Like shooting the wind." The Sheriff scratched his salt and pepper beard in thought. "We should talk to Pastor Riley. He might have some holy weapons of warfare for us."

Sarah sucked in some air when she heard this. "I don't like where this is headed at all."

"Aw, Mom, I'll make sure I'm careful."

Carson parroted, "Aw, Mom."

James smiled at Carson. "I'll be fine. I'll even have the pastor bless me against evil. I swear it." He held up a hand to complete the promise.

"No, I swear. I swear that if anything happens to my baby, then a ghostly gunman is the least of this town's worries." The comment was directed at Sheriff Axl Morgan, who pursed his lips in understanding.

"Let's get a move-on. We have a lot of work to do so we best see the Pastor and get started with preparations. A year can go by pretty quickly." Sheriff Morgan headed for the doors.

"A year? I'm not waiting a whole year for this fight." James grabbed the Sheriff's elbow. Sheriff Morgan looked down at James' grip and quickly removed his hand.

"Don't ever touch me like that, James. I don't like to be handled like a heifer at auction."

"Sorry, Sheriff."

"Now how do you suppose you're going to meet up with the gunslinger when he only shows himself once a year?"

"I'll lure him back."

"And how are you fixin' to do that?"

James looked around the saloon and then whispered to the Sheriff and his mother. "I don't know yet."

Sheriff Morgan sagged at James' response. Sarah slapped James on his backside. Then she pinched his ear and dragged him behind the Sheriff through the saloon doors. Carson giggled into his hand and followed along.

CHAPTER 15

"Over my dead body." Sarah shouted at James. Carson's eyes watered. Sarah watched Carson shrink under the table. He disliked arguments between Sarah and James. But none of them had ever gotten this loud before. She made a note to console Carson later.

"Jeez, Mom. You're treating me like a child. But I'm a man now."

"Who said you're a man? Did someone tell you that you were a man?"

James rolled his eyes. "I'm going to fight this thing and you can't stop me."

"If you walk out that door, then you are not welcome back here. Do you understand me?" She regretted the words as soon as they flew from her lips.

James continued to sharpen his knife. He pretended to ignore his mother but Sarah knew full well he was either biting his tongue or figuring out new ways to make his case. Sarah tried a softer approach. She sat next to James and brushed a hand over his hair.

"James, I can't lose you. You're all I have in this world." Again, she bit her lip as she noticed Carson lower his head. She knew he took that comment the wrong way. She loved him as if she had given birth to him. Sarah made another mental note for the follow-up consolation of Carson.

"How are you going to lose me? I beat Crouching Bear. And I'll beat the gunslinger." James' voice revealed he wasn't feeling as confident as the words he used.

"One doesn't equal the other. Crouching Bear was a real being. This...this ghost is not. It doesn't really exist...really." Sarah thought about that statement and then brushed it aside. "What happens if it doesn't go the way you want? Then what? What am I supposed to do? And who will be here for Carson?"

Carson quickly crawled out from under the table. He rushed over to them and pointed in James' face.

"You want to leave me?"

"I don't want to leave you, buddy."

"You leaved me for Crouching Bear. And now you leaved me for ghosts." Carson poked his finger in James' chest as he hammered home his accusation.

"Carson, I told you before. I didn't want you to get hurt by Crouching Bear. And this time, I'm not going anywhere. I'm gonna be right here in town."

Carson kicked James in the shin and ran back to the underside of the table. He buried his head in his arms and cried gently to himself. James shrugged at Carson's tears while he massaged his aching shin.

Sarah tried not to laugh. She thought Carson was so cute. He loved James and worshiped him. Sarah knew they would both do anything for each other. And she sympathized with Carson's fear and hurt feelings. She also knew James did things to protect Carson, even if Carson was too feeble to understand it.

"You see? Carson doesn't want you to do this either. Can't you reconsider it for him? For us?"

"That's low, Mom. How can you make me feel guilty about trying to help people?"

"Guilt is a mother's only weapon, sometimes."

"Well, too bad you can't guilt the gunslinger into going away."

"Watch your mouth, James. I'm still your mother."

"I know. I'm sorry."

Sarah stood up and went to the iron stove. She set a kettle of water upon it to make tea. She searched her heart for anything that could help sway her one way or the other. She was so torn between protecting her son and letting him spread his wings. James had grown up a lot over the last year. In many respects, he had become a man. But he was still too innocent for his own good. And he was always her little boy. Always would be.

"Look, this isn't easy for me either. What would you do if your child came to you and said they were going to go fight monsters and evil? Would you pat them on the back and send them on their way? Or would you try to talk them out of it?"

James seemed to consider her argument. He stopped sharpening the blade and he looked up at her with a serious face. "I guess I would do the same thing." He looked back down at the sharpening stone. "I would help him get ready and support him with all my heart."

"You trickster!" Sarah threw a dish towel at James. It never made it to his chair. James grinned with mischief. Sarah smiled back at him.

"What can I do, Mom? Help me do the right thing." James stood and approached Sarah. He held her hands in his. "I want to help people so bad. I want to be the hero. The one who saves the world from wrongdoing. But I'm scared too. And I'm not sure that I always make good decisions." He lowered his head.

Sarah let go of James' hands. She held his head. She felt the rough patches of whiskers on what used to be his baby-smooth face. "You do make some bad decisions. You get that from your father's side." James chuckled. "But it's okay to be unsure. And to make mistakes. That's what life is about. And growing up ain't easy. If it were, there would be no need for spankings and punishments."

James spun out of her grasp and went to the window. He stared through the glass in silence. Sarah followed him and rested her head on his shoulder. She realized James was tall enough now that she could do that. A year ago, she would have had to lean down to his shoulder a bit. Where had all the time gone, she asked herself.

"You have to do what you think is best, James. Nobody can make that decision for you. Not anymore." Sarah shed a tear as she relinquished herself to the inevitable. James was a man now. And no longer her own.

"Just keep in mind that if you do decide to go fight, I will disown you."

"Me too! I'll dizowned you."

Sarah smiled at Carson. She made another mental note. This time to thank Carson for taking her side.

CHAPTER 16

James grabbed several boxes of bullets and tossed them into the crate. He slid the crate across the wood floor with his foot. As he reached toward the coils of rope, Mr. Miller wandered up to him.

"Are you fixing to hog-tie the gunslinger, son?"

James realized Mr. Miller had a point. What good would a rope do against an apparition? "Yeah, I guess I should spend more time thinking about the supplies."

Mr. Miller bent over and plucked the boxes of bullets from the crate. He began to replace them on the shelf. "Then you'll probably want to re-think the need for bullets, too."

James sighed. "This fight is turning out to be a bit more complicated than I originally thought."

Mr. Miller folded his arms and turned to lean against the shelf. He sized up James. "James, I know you think this is something you have to do. But it's not. To hell with the people in town. You have to take care of yourself first."

James rolled his eyes, unable to contain his frustration. "Did my mother put you up to this? You can save your breath. She already ripped me to shreds."

Mr. Miller chuckled. "I haven't spoken to your mother, James. It's just common sense. Something we older folks have lots of. It usually grows in place of hair." He tapped his bald head while James laughed.

"It's not really about the people of town though. It's about me."

"How so?"

"Well, I believe I was born to become something big. A hero. And I just want my chance to prove it to the world; I am the hero I was meant to be."

"Prove it to the world? Or yourself?"

James sighed again. "Good question. I guess both."

"James, life is hard. Men face challenges each direction they turn. You know, it wasn't easy building this business. And it didn't work well right away. It took some years for me to get the store to turn a profit enough to subsist on."

"Really?"

"Sure, sure." Mr. Miller stood up straight. "And I had to make many decisions along the way. Now my decisions weren't as life and death as battling evil spirits. But, in a way, those decisions were just as important to determining whether I lived or died. Of starvation. Or by the hands of my creditors." He raised his eyebrows at James to complement his parable.

"So how did you get through it all?"

"I did what I thought was right, James. I could have turned a profit earlier if I had been more aggressive with sales. I could have made more money if I stocked only the items that sold most often. But I had a longer-term vision of what I wanted. I wanted a place where people can come find anything they might need. Anything, James. That took faith. Faith that people would see me for what I was." He paused to see if James would say something. James just stared at him so he continued. "That I was here for the long term. To help the community build and grow. Not to fill my pockets and then leave town."

"So what you're telling me is I need to do the right thing? And have a vision of what I want?"

"Yes. What do you want, James?"

"I want to help people. Save them from evil."

Mr. Miller chuckled. "Well, you certainly don't choose small goals, do you?"

"I guess not, sir."

"So what the hell are you doing working in my store?"

"I want to support my family and provide for them."

"And that is doing the right thing."

"Does this mean that fighting the haunted gunslinger is NOT the right thing?"

Mr. Miller rubbed his forehead. "I don't think you're getting my point. Look here, you have to follow your heart and your gut. As long as you do the right thing, then the good Lord will take care of the rest."

"My heart tells me to rid this town of that ghost. But my gut tells me to take care of my family and forget about dangerous spirits." James stared at his boots.

"That's why life is hard, James." Mr. Miller rested his hand on James' shoulder.

"So what should I do?"

Miller laughed louder. "I can tell you what to do when you are stocking my shelves and sweeping my floors, James. But not out there." He pointed out the window. "Out there, you're on your own. A free man. Free to make good choices and bad. And free to live with the consequences of each decision."

"Jeez, Mr. Miller. I'm more confused now than I was when I came in here." James scratched his head.

"Good. Now get out of my store."

"What?"

"You heard me, James. Get the hell out of my store." Mr. Miller's tone suggested he was serious.

"But why?"

"Because you are no longer my employee, James. You're fired."

James' jaw dropped. His eyebrows shot up to the top of his face as he begged to understand what had just happened.

"But, sir. What did I do?"

"I don't hire ghost hunters and vigilantes, James. It's not good for business. And for me? It's not the right thing to do."

"I thought we were having a good chat, Mr. Miller. I'm sorry if I upset you."

"I'm not upset, James. It's just business. I have mine and you have yours. Now take your business elsewhere." Mr. Miller pointed at the front door with finality.

"But...I...I..."

"You're a man, James. Isn't that what you said at the meeting?"

James nodded.

"Then act like one."

James shuffled slowly down the aisle. He glanced at Mr. Miller, who busied himself with a stack of papers at the counter, never once lifting his eyes to meets James.

James felt deflated. What just happened? How did everything turn upside down in such a short period of time? Yesterday he had a good-paying job. He was safe and happy in this nice little town. And now this. He was cast aside by the townspeople. Then his mother and Carson. And now Mr. Miller.

James had an urge to cry but the words kept repeating in his mind. Act like one. Act like one. Act like one.

He shut the door and stood on the front porch of the general store. The sun felt hot against his cheeks. James lowered the brim of his hat and walked away.

CHAPTER 17

James peeked in the window. It looked somewhat dark inside because the sunshine gleamed along the panes. Suddenly, a face appeared on the other side of the glass. James screamed in fright. Miss Lark smiled and waved him inside.

As James opened the school's door, Miss Lark hurried around the classroom with a broom. "James. Come in."

He shut the door behind him. He took several steps between some desks and realized it had been some time since he had last set foot in a schoolhouse. The desks seemed much smaller than he had remembered them. He thought of sitting at one of the desks and then figured he wouldn't fit now that he was grown up.

"What brings you here, James?" Miss Lark brushed a blond curl back behind her ear. The blue dress she wore was very form-fitting and James couldn't help but admire her figure. She was fairly young, even though she was clearly older than James. Yet, she had a woman's shape. And James liked it.

"Um…I guess I had nowhere else to go."

Miss Lark stopped sweeping and shot James a sour look. "Well, don't you know how to make a woman feel nice."

James removed his hat and looked at his boots. "Sorry. I didn't mean it like that." He walked over to the long bench along the wall and sat down. James placed his hat on the bench and lowered his head into his hands.

Miss Lark rested the broom against her desk and approached James. She took a seat on the bench next to him. "Sounds like you aren't too happy today. Did someone in jail call you a bad name?"

James laughed at her gentle ribbing. "No. I haven't been in jail today. Yet." He looked into her eyes. They were greenish with some light brown specks. James wondered how she could have such different eyes from everyone he had ever met before.

"Well that's good. I wouldn't want to have to fight your mother again."

"Yeah, sorry about that. My Mom can be pretty protective of me. Us. Protective of us." He quickly corrected his phrase before Miss Lark could question why he didn't include Carson in her protective nature.

Miss Lark giggled and brushed her curl back again. "Mothers know best, I suppose. I guess I'll learn that myself someday." Her cheeks blushed as she made the comment. She bit her lower lip.

"Miss Lark..."

"Please. Call me Eleanor." She rested her hand on James' knee. He felt something stir in his pants suddenly. He tried to picture drowned puppies and now it was his turn to blush.

"Okay. Eleanor. I feel lost."

"Maybe I can help find you. Why don't you pick up the broom and give me a hand while we chat."

James reddened even more. He wasn't sure he could stand up right now without embarrassing himself. He rubbed his forehead and closed his eyes tight. James pictured his mother yelling at him last night about fighting the gunslinger. Immediately, he was in good shape to stand up.

"This is going to sound strange. But...did you ever know deep inside that you were meant for something...and that you had to do it no matter what?"

"Sure. When I was a little girl, my mother read books to me every day. I loved the sound of the words and the paintings they created in my mind. I knew right away that I wanted to be a teacher."

James stopped sweeping and leaned on the broom. "Sort of, I guess. Anyway, the part of me that knows I have to do what I have to do is battling the part of me that is afraid to do what I have to do."

Eleanor stared at James as she tried to follow along.

"And then there's the stuff that others want me to do or think I should do, which I do want to do, but on account of what I have to do and I know I have to do…"

"James. James. Please. I am getting a headache trying to comprehend all this. What are you saying?"

James huffed and leaned against her desk. He liked Miss Lark, Eleanor, but he didn't want to tell her everything. He was afraid she would think he was weird. James whispered to himself that he was being silly. Did he really think a woman like Miss Lark would be interested in a boy like him?

"I want to fight the gunslinger. I have to do it. But nobody else wants me to."

Eleanor nodded. "So watching the Mayor get shot right before you, and getting grazed by a bullet yourself wasn't enough to scare you away?"

"Oddly, no."

She came closer to James. He could smell her skin. It had a lavender scent. James' head swirled as he tried to focus on his dilemma.

"What does your mother want you to do?"

"She wants me to stay home and do nothing." James folded his arms in frustration as he glanced out the window.

"I have to agree with your mother on this one, James."

"What? But I thought you spoke for me?"

"I did. I represented your interests in the fact that you had nothing to do with the Mayor's death. And that you didn't belong in jail. It would hurt me if…" Eleanor paused. "It would be tragic if you were to get hurt or die." She turned away from James and shuffled some things on the table between the windows.

"You know, this was the one place I thought I could go when everyone else threw me out. My Mom, Mr. Miller, now you." James stomped a foot like a petulant child.

"Mr. Miller?"

"Yeah. He fired me this morning on account of me being a vigilante." He felt like he might cry but he swallowed it down. Real men don't cry, he chided. "Maybe it was a mistake moving to this town."

Eleanor got closer to James. Her eyes darted back and forth as she searched his face. "I just want what's best for you, James."

"What's best for me is to leave this place. Any man would be a fool to stay where he ain't wanted." He grabbed his hat off the bench and placed it on his head. James stormed off toward the door. As he opened it, Eleanor stopped him.

"James?"

He pivoted to face her. "Yeah?"

"Isn't."

"Huh?"

"Where he ISN'T wanted."

James huffed and slammed the door closed.

CHAPTER 18

Carson shuffled the deck of cards as he watched Sarah leave the room. He was relieved that it was over. Carson was afraid he was going to lose control. The cards sliding between his fingers soothed him.

He wished James was here right now. Carson missed him. He didn't like to spend prolonged periods of time away from James. Sometimes, when James went to work at the store, Carson would get so lonely he would try to start a fire in the room. Even though he didn't really know how to do it. And then, just in the nick of time, James would come home for lunch. Or dinner. And everything would go back to normal.

Today was more difficult. Sarah talked. A long time. Carson struggled so hard to pay attention. His mind went to so many places. His legs wiggled like they wanted to jump up and run around the room. His fingers twitched, longing to grasp the solid deck of cards. To feel the crisp edges along his fingertips.

Sarah had spent most of the time worrying out loud to Carson about James. She believed in his abilities and determination, she said. But she was afraid of something bad happening to James. She said she wanted to let James make his own decisions and mistakes. What scared her most was that if he made a mistake this time, it could cost James his life.

When Sarah mentioned the possibility of James dying, Carson found it easier to concentrate. His focus seemed to sharpen as he tried to figure out how to help James. Carson wouldn't let any type of boogiedman hurt his bestest friend in the whole world. Nothin' doin'. Carson aimed to stand up for James. He wanted to punch out the boogiedman like James punched out Mr. Black with his forehead.

Carson splayed the cards on the wood floor in front of him. He set them up to play solitaire even though poker was his favorite. Well, it was his favorite when he beat James. He giggled to himself as he recalled the multitude of losing expressions on James' face. Carson loved to beat James at cards.

He didn't understand why Sarah thanked him for taking her side. He hadn't taken anything from her. She seemed to be pleased with him for it so he didn't spend too much time trying to figure it out.

Carson scooped up the cards again. He got up and walked to the window, leaving the deck of cards on the table as he went. The street below was busy with people and wagons. He found it hard to believe it was the same street that had emptied for the gunslinger.

He pulled his finger from his belt loop, pretending it was a six shooter. Each time he drew it, Carson aimed his finger across the street and made a gunshot sound with his mouth. After a few rounds, he used the back of his sleeve to dry off all the spit on his lips.

Carson remembered how he was worried too. He was afraid James would try to leave him behind again. Carson still felt a little sore at James for last time, even though he hadn't said anything to James about it. He knew James tried to protect him against danger. But they were supposed to be a team. Riding together on adventures. Fighting bad guys and getting newspaper stories about them. Together. It's how they dreamed it out loud over meals. And in their favorite hiding spot.

He traced the window pane with his small finger. The smooth surface of the wood reminded him of the feel of the playing cards. The edges felt the same when he held a deck.

Carson was determined to help James fight the gunslinger. But how? Sarah would do her best to keep Carson indoors. And James would shelter Carson from getting involved. He knew James would try to ditch him again. So what else could he do to help out? If nobody would listen to him or let him help, he would have to do it on his own.

He turned and headed to the cupboard. The drawer for the silverware slid easily. In the notch on the left sat a handful of steak knives. Carson reached down and picked up the first knife. The blade was a little dull. He rested the knife aside and went through the remaining knives. They all seemed to be dull. He ran his finger along the blade and it sliced his finger open. A line of blood traced his fingerprint and then it swelled.

Carson said "ouch" out loud to the empty room. He dropped the knife on the floor and grabbed a dishtowel from the linen drawer. He wrapped the towel around his bloody finger and squeezed it tight. He remembered how his mommy had done the same thing once when he fell down the saloon stairs and scraped up his knees. She came to his aid and dabbed a rag on the wounds. When they kept bleeding, she told him to wrap the rag around the scrapes and squeeze it tight until the boo-boo went away. He remembered how it worked like magic.

Carson thought of his mommy. He wondered when she was going to come home. He felt a little guilty for forgetting about her. So much had happened since she had left town to take care of a sick relative. And he had almost forgotten what she looked like now. He wanted to cry about it but he had things to do. He still had to figure out how to get the gunslinger.

Leaving the dishtowel around his hand, Carson went back to the knife he had dropped. He scooped it up and turned the blade around in the sunlight streaming through the window. Carson knew how to sharpen a knife. He had watched James do it countless times. He found James' sharpening stone. He sat on the floor under the table and began working on the blade. Once he got it sharp enough, he could stab the gunslinger and save James and the town.

Carson grinned to himself as he imagined the adventure. He got excited about it because, if he won, James would trust him enough to include him on every adventure. And Sarah would let Carson out of the room more often. He couldn't wait.

"Back to square one," Carson whispered to himself.

CHAPTER 19

James ran his hand through his messy hair. Sheriff Axl Morgan sat behind his large desk, staring at James. The meeting didn't start off on the right foot.

"Let me get this straight. Your plan for tackling this evil ghost is to call him names?"

"Sort of. Well, not exactly, I guess. When I said I wanted to tease it, I meant, you know, try to get it to show itself by making it angry."

"Are you out of your mind, son?" The Sheriff seemed exasperated. "What makes you think that yelling at a wicked spirit is gonna bring it back to life?" He slammed a fist on the desk, which rattled the few items atop the plateau.

James blew air out of his mouth and sat back against the chair. He searched for better words to describe his plan, but he was drawing blanks. And if he didn't think of something fast, his plan would be over in a flash like a stick of dynamite in an iron mine.

"The way I see it, the gunslinger said he would come back for me. And he knew my name. So…if I call on him at high noon, then maybe he'll come back."

"Even if you were to whistle Dixie for this ghost and he were to magically appear based on your toot-sweet sounds, then what the hell would you do? Draw down on him and shoot it out in the streets?"

"I haven't figured that out yet."

Sheriff Morgan rocked back in his chair and let out a slow whistle. "Impressive, James. I put my neck on the line for you and this is the best you got? Schoolhouse bullying and 'I don't know yet'?"

James looked down in embarrassment.

"These folks are counting on me to clean up this mess. And I swore to them you and I had a plan to do it. It's all that saved your neck from the swinging rope. And my tenure is at stake now that I vouched for your backside." The Sheriff stood up and walked a small circle behind his desk. James watched him pace with his hands resting on his gun belt.

"I can do this, Sheriff. I know I can."

"Do what? Talk out your crap-hole? Promise things you can't back up?"

James stood. He put his hat on his head. "Well, if you don't want to help me, Sheriff, that's just fine. I'll do it myself." He turned for the door.

"Sit your ass down, son." The shout shook the window panes and startled James. He stopped dead in his tracks and faced the Sheriff. "Sit. Now."

James plopped back into the hard wooden chair. He lowered the brim of his hat to shield himself from a barrage of cuss words and screaming which he fully expected.

"Sorry I lost my temper, James." Sheriff Morgan sighed and sat back down behind his desk. "It's not easy keeping a town safe. Sometimes I fear the townspeople more than the occasional gang of miscreants. Or ghosts."

James nodded even though he had no idea what 'miscreants' meant.

Sheriff Morgan came around the desk and sat against the edge. With folded arms, he gazed down at the top of James' hat. "We're gonna have to clear out the people. That's for sure. The hardest part is what to do when the gunslinger shows himself."

James looked up at the Sheriff. From his vantage point, there seemed to be more age and wrinkles in the Sheriff's face than he realized before.

"Well, if bullets don't work, I guess knives won't either." James rubbed his jaw and then jumped up with excitement. "I know. We'll trap it."

"Trap it?"

"Yeah, trap it. Lure the gunslinger out of hiding. And then, BANG, right into a trap."

"Like a genie in a magic lantern?" The Sheriff mocked the idea sarcastically.

"Not exactly. But sort of. If I can get the gunslinger stuck in a trap, then maybe I can remove it from town."

Sheriff Morgan rolled his eyes. "And even if it worked, what would you use to trap it in?"

"Uh…a mirror. Yeah, a mirror. Aren't mirrors supposed to be the windows to the spirit side?"

"I don't know where you get your tales from, son. But I never heard that before."

"Well, I heard it or read it. I can't remember now. But, if spirits can enter our world through mirrors, they must be able to get trapped in them too." James couldn't contain his excitement. He felt like he had a plan now and that gave him new energy.

Sheriff Morgan stared at James. "Well, at least it's something, I reckon. We better get started then. I'll work on getting folks out of town for a few hours. I'm sure that won't be easy." He stood and picked up his hat from the desk. "You work on getting a mirror and we'll meet back here in a bit. We need to get this done tomorrow. High noon. Understood?"

James nodded. He immediately thought of Carson. How could he get the boy to agree to leave town? His mother would back him up since she would not let harm come to Carson. But James didn't want to let his little buddy down. He had promised they would fight evil together. And he was fixing to leave the boy behind yet again. Some friend, James admonished himself.

Sheriff Morgan set his hat upon his head. He opened the door and swung his arm out to indicate James should exit first. James smiled and set off across the street.

His plan was to find a mirror first. There were several large mirrors in the brothel for the ladies to dress in. The trick would be to grab a mirror without his mother knowing. If she didn't approve of his battling the gunslinger, she probably wouldn't approve of him borrowing an expensive mirror either. Then he would have to talk to Carson. James figured he would rather go up against the haunted gunslinger than disappoint Carson.

James thought to himself that this hero business had lots of downsides. Every time he thought he was beyond an obstacle, another one would take its place.

He scuffed his boots in the dirt, narrowly missing something a horse had recently left behind.

CHAPTER 20

Sarah watched James from behind the dressing blind. She snickered to herself how funny he was. But she was still going to let him have it.

James had come into the common room of the brothel on tip toes. He had peered around the corner and checked the hallway several times to make sure the coast was clear. Little did he know that his mother was tidying up inside. When she saw him enter the room, she decided to hop behind the dressing blind to see what he was up to.

Sarah stifled another giggle. She couldn't help herself. She felt like a little girl again, hiding from a friend so she could jump out and scare them. Except this time, she was hiding from James. And she planned to jump out and give him a scare too. One that he would never forget.

James approached the full-size mirror which stood on wooden legs on the other side of the dressing blind. Sarah heard him grunting as he attempted to lift the mirror up. She peeked over the blind and noticed his red face as he turned with the mirror in his arms.

"Stop right there." She shouted over the blind. James shrieked and lunged forward. His body cradled the mirror as he sprawled out on the floor. She was impressed that he had the wherewithal to twist his body so that he ended up underneath the mirror, saving it from breaking.

"Mom." James shouted back at her.

Sarah sauntered from behind the dressing blind. She walked up to James who was frozen on the floor.

"There's no need to take the mirror out of the room. You can check yourself out right here." She raised her eyebrows so James knew he was caught in the act.

"I…um…just…"

"Knock it off, James. What do you think you are doing with my mirror?" She rested her hands on her hips and tapped her foot.

"Let me explain."

"Well, I'm waiting. Aren't I?"

James rolled gently over and placed the mirror on the floor. He brushed himself off while he stood to face his mother.

"You see. I need to borrow the mirror to trap the ghost." He winced, expecting her to yell.

"So you're going through with it, huh?" She didn't wait for a response. "Then I guess this is it."

James grabbed her arm as Sarah began to storm off.

"Wait, Mom. Please."

Sarah paused to face him. She was so torn. James was a young man and she knew he was free to make his own choices now. But she feared for his life and struggled with her maternal instincts. She knew she wouldn't be able to just turn it off after seventeen plus years.

"I have to do this. You know I do. And the mirror is gonna help me trap the gunslinger so we can get him out of town. I'll pay you for the mirror. Honest."

"Well if you're borrowing it, why would you have to pay me?"

"On account of I will have to break it."

"What? Why?"

"Once the ghost is in the mirror, I have to take it out to the fields and shatter it. Then the ghost won't have a way back to this side."

Sarah groaned. "James, that is an expensive mirror." She huffed at him.

"I need some help too." He scrunched his shoulders to accentuate his begging. Sarah shifted from one foot to the other without responding. She waited to hear his next request.

"I need you to talk to Carson for me."

"Oh, no. No way. I am not doing your dirty work for you, James. I cleaned your britches but I ain't cleaning up your messes anymore." She stormed for the door.

James chased her into the hallway. "Mom. Please. I can't disappoint him again. You gotta help me out with this. He'll listen to you. I don't want him to get upset."

Sarah spun around as James slammed into her. "And you think he won't be upset when I break the bad news to him? Are you insane? That boy wants to be like you more than anything in the world. And all you can do is run off on him and leave him behind. How could you, James? You were the one who promised to look out for him."

James lowered his head. "I know. But I didn't know that I would get these chances to fight bad guys."

"Funny. Because you dreamed about it for years and got Carson all caught up in your delusions. And now you want to toss him aside."

James' expression changed. "You mean it's okay if I take him along with me."

"Hell no! I didn't say that at all. What I am saying is you should stay put and forget about ghosts and start taking care of your duties. You have a job and a family to care for."

"I lost my job."

Sarah fumed. She couldn't believe how much things had changed with James. He seemed to have been growing up and taking on more responsibilities. And now it was all crashing down around him. And her.

"James, I want you to take that damn mirror and go do whatever it is you feel a calling to do. But don't come back here. You can't keep hurting Carson. And you can't hurt me either. I won't allow it." She sighed and gently kissed his cheek. "Good luck, James. I will miss you."

Sarah walked away and left James standing, dejected, in the hallway. He watched her go. His shoulders slumped as he turned to retrieve the mirror from the common room. The sound of his shuffling boots echoed a sorrowful cadence.

Underneath a small couch in the hallway, Carson hid. The small boy quietly cried to himself as he overheard James' plan to leave him behind yet again. He put his head on his hands and stayed there for a few more hours.

CHAPTER 21

James carried the mirror across the dusty street. His lungs strained with the effort of hauling it for so long. He had fumbled to get the mirror down the stairs from the brothel. And then he had begun the long trek from the saloon to the Sheriff's office on the other side of town.

He set the mirror down in one of the last clear spots of roadway. The street was riddled with horse droppings and James struggled to carry the heavy structure while avoiding the excrement clumps. James tried to catch his breath for a moment. He looked around at the busy street.

James couldn't help but notice the reaction from his fellow townspeople. Half the folks ignored him as if he didn't exist. The rest leered at him with contempt or whispered to their neighbors while staring at him. He felt the hatred as the vibes traveled in his direction.

He lifted the heavy mirror again and took two steps before nearly colliding with Eleanor. James almost dropped the mirror. He stared at her as he tried to figure out if she was going to give him more grief.

"Hello, James."

"Hi."

"That's an awfully large mirror."

"And heavy too." He brushed a sleeve across his sweaty forehead. His hat bumped up accidentally.

"Would you like a hand?"

"Uh, no thanks. I can do it."

Eleanor nodded and looked to the side. She brought her gaze back to James.

"I hope you forgive me for yesterday. I didn't mean to upset you."

James breathed a sigh of relief. Maybe he wasn't going to find himself in trouble after all. A first, he whispered to himself.

"So what brings you out here?"

"I wanted to talk to you and your mother said you were headed this way. She seemed pretty upset." Eleanor squinted, with the sun in her eyes, to look at James.

"Well, she ain't the only one with hurt feelings." As soon as he said it, James winced for whining.

"I know you want to save everyone from the gunslinger. But it's not your responsibility."

James' face soured for the coming onslaught.

"I think you're brave. Most men pretend to be tough. But they really aren't."

James stuck his chest out. "Yeah, well I'm a man now so…" He didn't know where he was going with his bravado so the sentence just trailed off awkwardly like a fart in church.

Eleanor giggled. "I just thought you should know that I am on your side, regardless what you choose to do."

James felt butterflies in his gut. His heart pounded and he began to feel a slight stir in his dungarees. He had to picture Mr. Miller's bald head to keep his excitement at bay.

"I would like to invite you to my home for dinner. You know, once you defeat the gunslinger. That is, if you had an inclination to eat something. Or…something." Eleanor bit her lip to stop herself.

"Um, yeah. I guess. Sure, I can eat. I mean, I like to eat. Uh, that would be fine." Sweat beaded up on his upper lip, but not from the heat. He was becoming increasingly more nervous.

The silence between them was charged. Eleanor turned her head towards Clip's Barber Shop, for no good reason. James faced the other way as he watched a man enter the General Store. Eleanor caught Mrs.

Thompson's eye. The elder woman shook her head in disapproval. Eleanor blushed and turned her attention back to James.

"It's settled then. Dinner. My house."

James nodded. "Ayup." He squinted in horror as his nervousness caused him to combine 'uh-huh' with 'yup'. "I gotta go now." He blurted out and scooped up the heavy mirror with a burst of energy. He heard Eleanor say "Bye" from behind him but he kept moving.

When he arrived at the Sheriff's office, James set down the large mirror. He gasped for air. He hadn't realized he had held his breath the rest of the way over. James removed his hat and fanned some air into his flushed face. He looked around for Eleanor but she was gone. He sighed in relief that the whole encounter was over.

James tried the door to the Sheriff's office but it was locked. He decided to wait for the Sheriff to return. He didn't want to leave the mirror unattended. Even sitting before the Sheriff's office, he knew the mirror would disappear with some handsy passerby. James sat on a dusty stool and watched the street full of people.

Suddenly, a man on a horse screamed at James from down the street. He sat up straight as the rider neared. James wondered what the man could want and why he had to shout so loud, creating a scene. The man spat a wad of chaw as he tugged the horse's reins.

"Whatcha wanna blind ever'one?"

"Huh?"

"I said, whatcha wanna blind ever'one? That dang looking glass is burnin' my eyes clear across the town." The man pointed at the mirror with a long, dirty fingernail.

James glanced at the mirror and realized it was reflecting the sun light to a focused point down the street. "Oh, sorry, Mister. I didn't mean to cause you any trouble." He tipped his hat to the rider and busied himself turning the mirror toward the office.

"Next time be more careful 'afore I give ya a whippin'."

James spun around. "No need to get all sore, fella. I said I was sorry. And I'm moving the mirror, aren't I?" James was surprised at how quick the sass shot out of his mouth. It dawned on him that his temper kept showing itself now that he had gotten involved in all these high-stress situations.

"Eh, if that there ghost weren't gonna kill ya, I'd hop down from this here horse and do it myself." He spat again.

"You could try." James did it again. But he wasn't about to be threatened by some dirty rider who didn't live in town. The guy was here on business and James figured he didn't owe the man anything.

The rider's eyes opened wide and he slid out of the saddle. As he tied up his horse, James tossed his hat on the stool and started rolling up his sleeves. The man was a little bit bigger than him but James didn't care. He just wanted to land one set of knuckles on the guy's nose and the beating would then be worth it.

Just then, a huge hand clutched James' shoulder. It was the Sheriff.

"Best be on your way, Mister."

The rider stopped in his tracks. His eyes darted from James to the Sheriff's badge and back to James.

"This must be yer lucky day, boy. Guess I'll leave ya ta the ghostly gunslinger anyhows." He took a step back. "Can't wait fer yer funeral." He tipped his hat. "Sheriff."

James watched the man untie his horse and climb up. The man grinned a toothless grin at James and galloped away. James turned to face Sheriff Morgan. The Sheriff shook his head and laughed under his breath. James heard him say, "You got some acorns, kid."

CHAPTER 22

James setup the mirror in the middle of the street, about fifty yards in front of the clock tower. He draped a wool blanket over it. When the time was right, James planned to remove the blanket so the gunslinger would see his reflection. He hoped it would work because there was no alternate plan.

The street was empty. The sound of the wind created an eerie whoosh that swept along the wooden porches and funneled to the end of town. James glanced up at the clock tower. It showed ten minutes to noon. There was no turning back. James swallowed a lump of saliva.

Sheriff Morgan showed up. He held his Winchester rifle in one hand, pointing the muzzle at the reddish soil.

"Any final thoughts?"

James swallowed again. "Yeah, can I go home?"

The Sheriff chuckled. "That's funny." He tilted his hat brim back, revealing crow's feet at the corners of his eyes. "You call him out and then trigger the trap. I'll back you up from the rooftop above Miller's." He pointed to the perch with the barrel of the rifle.

"What good is backing me up with a gun? I thought the bullets passed through him last time?"

"They did."

"So, what then?"

"Maybe it will be different this time. You know. When he catches his reflection."

"What if it isn't different this time?"

"Then I'll be in position to end it for you…before you suffer."

James' jaw dropped. He didn't like the sound of that. He had already been awake all night, contemplating his potential death today. But the finality of the backup bullet to put him out of his misery made it all too real. James wondered if he had time to evacuate his bowels.

Sheriff Morgan smiled at James and punched his shoulder. "Look at the bright side, kid. In ten minutes, it'll all be over. One way or another."

James tried to nod but he was frozen from his skull to his boots.

The Sheriff shook James out of his funk with more instructions on timing and positioning. They ran through their gear checks and wished each other luck.

"Keep your chin up, James. At least you had the courage to stand up and do something. Unlike the rest of the town." Sheriff Morgan patted James on the shoulder and turned to leave. He stopped and looked at James again. "You are one of a kind, James. Regardless of what happens today, nobody can take anything away from you. You took a chance to save these people. Live or die, you're a hero in my books." Sheriff Morgan walked off.

James watched the Sheriff with tears in his eyes. His heart throbbed with pride that he was recognized for his bravery. Within seconds, he went from self-doubt to realizing his dream come true. Somebody considered him a hero. Isn't that what he had always wanted? Didn't he dream and strive to reach a moment like this? His thoughts reverted back to Crouching Bear and the epic battle. People patted him on the back and called him hero when he had returned to town. But it hadn't hit home like the Sheriff's comments. Maybe he was too shell-shocked from his maiden journey. Or too exhausted.

James wiped some tears from his cheeks with the back of his sleeve. He gazed at the sky to take in the calm blueness. Cottony clouds drifted by without knowledge of the impending fight. The serenity of the heavens washed over James. He felt inconsequential on the precipice of this major event. He realized the sky would still be blue tomorrow. The sun would still shine. The universe didn't care about James or these townspeople.

He took one more look around the town. The windows were empty. Doors were locked down. Just James and the dusty breeze were all that breathed at this moment. James glanced up at the clock tower and the minute hand paused, a few strikes before noon. His heart palpitated and he found himself trying to catch his breath as the present fused with the past.

His hand wandered to the back of his belt loop. The warm gun handle gave him comfort, even if it was useless against a spirit. Better to have than not to have, he thought. He pulled the pistol out and inspected the cylinder. Spinning it in his fingers, he counted the six rounds nestled inside. He replaced the gun in his belt and patted the handle twice to show his respect for his protector.

The wool blanket draped over the mirror bristled in the gentle breeze. A gust surged and the end of the blanket flared up, revealing the lower side of the mirror perched upon the wooden legs. James smoothed the blanket down to keep it from flying away. The breeze abated.

James glanced back at the clock. One minute to noon. He turned on his heels and faced the desolate street. He took a deep breath and cracked his finger knuckles. He knew there was no turning back now. The hour had arrived and he had to answer for the promises he had made.

The saliva in James' mouth dried up and he swallowed a gulp of air. He wished he had a drink of water or something to bring his mouth back to life.

The clock chimed.

James dug his boot heels into the soil. His eyes scanned the avenue for movement.

Dong!

His mind drew a blank as he tried to recall what he had planned to say to elicit the gunslinger.

Dong!

A crow cawed and flew off, almost as if it sensed a presence. An unseen evil.

Dong!

James stole a glance out of the corner of his eye to the roof of Miller's General Store. He knew it was strange, but he didn't want to divulge the Sheriff's position in case the gunslinger watched him.

Dong!

James tried to remember how many times the clock had chimed. He lost count and now felt like he would be caught off guard if he couldn't be prepared to spring into action.

Dong!

Dang it, how many was that? James screamed at himself in his mind.

Dong!

Each chime echoed between the barren edifices, making the sound more ominous.

CHAPTER 23

The saloon was packed. It was practically standing room only as the townspeople waited for the show. When the Sheriff had told everyone to leave town for a few hours, a contingent of people chose to stay, regardless of the danger involved. They swore to Sheriff Morgan they would congregate in the saloon only, thus minimizing their exposure. Sheriff Morgan argued against it but in the end he relented. There were just too many rebels to lock up in his small jail. So he told them they stayed at their own risk. The only person who was excited was the undertaker.

Sarah was stuffed in the middle of the mob. She glanced over at Miss Lark, who chewed a fingernail in the back corner of the bar. Sarah snickered to herself since Miss Lark appeared to be dressed in her best outfit. She thought the woman was strikingly beautiful. But she wasn't ready to hand over James to her. Not yet.

The saloon was silent. Nobody uttered a word as they nervously awaited the showdown. The only sound was an occasional clink of a mug or a stifled cough. Each individual acted as if the slightest noise might attract the gunslinger's attention their way. And nobody was willing to risk it.

Sarah had fought to get this far through the crowd. She eventually gave up since it was just too dense to wriggle toward the front. She desperately wanted a front row seat so she could keep her motherly eyes on her son. The more she contemplated it, this spot in the middle of the crowd would be better. If James were to be killed, she would rather hear about it from the folks than witness it herself. She hoped that wouldn't be the case. But she was extremely worried about James' chances. After all, he was taking on a ghost. Not a flesh and blood being that could be overcome or conquered. A ghost. An ethereal spirit that couldn't be seen nor hurt by human hands. A bead of sweat formed along her forehead.

Sarah made eye contact with several patrons. Some folks nodded silently at her to acknowledge her family's valor and sacrifice on their behalf. A few others grimaced or snarled in her direction. Even as James risked everything to help them, they despised him for existing. She made a mental note of the men who treated her in this fashion. She would be sure to set them with the fattest and ugliest whores in the brothel. Sarah thought to herself that it was little solace to control their sexual pleasure. But it was something she could hang on to.

She realized that Carson was no longer by her side. He had clung to her as she made her way through the mob. Somewhere along the way she had gotten too distracted to recognize he was gone. Sarah twisted her neck to search the heads around her. It was no use, she thought. Carson was too small and she would never find him in this sea of filthy humanity. She ached to call out his name but, if she did, she knew the saloon would react harshly. She wiggled herself lower to attempt to peer through the arms and legs of the crowd. A man alongside Sarah leaned into her with all his weight. Apparently he wasn't pleased with the nudging of her body. He kept the pressure up until she squeezed his nuts through his trousers. Sarah placed a gentle but firm grip on them. He got the message and backed away as far as he could. She winked at him sarcastically.

Beneath all the human cargo, Sarah struggled to find Carson. Between dusty chaps and hoop skirts, every nook and cranny was filled. She gave up and raised herself to a normal level. She thought briefly about shouting Carson's name. Her senses returned and she bit her lower lip to maintain her composure.

Sarah wondered if Carson had slinked off to the back of the bar. He was a shy child at times. It may have been caused by all the times he had been mistreated or teased for being slow. It was sad how mean people could be, she thought. And it wasn't just children who picked on him and called him names. It was adults too. Grown adults who went to church each Sunday to worship a God who taught them to love one another and treat others as you would have them treat you. Yet, they abused the boy as if he were sub-human, and not protected by the same God that took care of them. Sarah clenched her fists as she reflected on the hypocrisy of them all.

The clock tower chimed.

A shock wave of stiffening spread through the crowd. Each person tensed for the coming battle. Sarah's stomach shot up to her throat and back down again. She began to pray for James. She glanced at Miss Lark. The woman just stared back at her with wide eyes. Fear etched along her mouth.

Sarah wished she could see James one more time. What if she never saw him alive again? She had given him a quick hug and kiss this morning because she didn't like long goodbyes. In hindsight, Sarah wished she had held him just a little longer. Memories of James as a baby and toddler flashed before her eyes.

Dong!

Tears filled Sarah's eyes no matter how hard she strained to avoid them. Sarah was scared about how much time was left before James would win or lose…his life.

Silence filled the air. Not one person made a sound. But the crowd leaned ever so slightly toward the windows and doorway. The echo of the chimes replayed in Sarah's ears. Her brain tried to fill in the gaps where there was once sound.

Her heart pounded so hard she thought everyone around her could hear it.

CHAPTER 24

Silence.

Nothing moved.

Even the breeze had dissipated.

James scanned the street for signs of the gunslinger. He was all alone and the hairs on the back of his neck stood up. An electric charge hung in the air.

He licked his dry lips with an even drier tongue. James noticed the sweat on his forehead and upper lip. His eyes darted back and forth for movement.

Nothing.

"I'm here." James croaked to the emptiness.

He waited and still nothing stirred.

James decided to speak up this time. "I said, I'm here." He looked around. "Show yourself or forever be banished from this town."

Silence.

James wanted to look up at Sheriff Morgan but was too paranoid to tip his hand. He took a shaky step forward.

"I'm not afraid of you, gunslinger." He heard the quaver in his voice.

A disturbance formed up the street. Crackling static broke the silence. Small flashes of light popped several times and then a shape took form within the flashes. The shape was hazy at first and then filled slowly with color. It was the gunslinger.

James gulped. The much anticipated confrontation had arrived. He felt a need to empty his bladder but chose to ignore it. The black eyes felt like they cut holes through James' soul. A shudder ran down his spine.

"I told you I would come back for you, James." The haunted gunslinger's creaky voice was barely above a whisper. James heard it all the same.

The gunslinger swung his long, leather duster open and tucked the tails behind his six shooters. The gnarled, bony hands perched upon the handles. The shiny silver of the guns glinted in the sun.

"You're scared." The words sounded in James' head. The gunslinger's lips never moved.

"I'm not scared." James spoke defiantly.

"Sure you are. I feel your blood pumping through your veins, kid." Again, the words were in his head, as if he had spoken them himself.

"What do you want, gunslinger?"

"I want what everyone wants. Respect."

"You're dead so how are people supposed to respect you?"

"That's where you're wrong, James. I am very much alive."

James narrowed his eyes. "Well, if you're alive, then how come you disappear?"

The gunslinger laughed out loud. The laugh sounded like sand gurgled in its throat. "I like to travel around, man."

"Suppose I say you have our respect now. Will you leave these good people alone?"

The gunslinger's wide smile faded. He took two steps forward, the spurs clinking beneath him. He played with his thin, black mustache. "Don't reckon these people are that good, James. And respect is just a start."

James was confused but he wanted to show the gunslinger that he was in control. He cleared his throat. "What else then?"

"Revenge, James. Revenge."

"Revenge for what?"

The gunslinger placed his hands back on his pistols. He lifted them and spun them around his bony fingers like lightning. Before James knew it, the guns had been re-holstered. The gunslinger's smile spread.

"Do you believe, James?"

"Believe in what?"

"The afterlife."

James reflected on his days in church. It had been awhile since he had last gone to services. He wished he had been going all along. It might have provided an extra barrier of protection.

"I believe in heaven. And hell."

The gunslinger adjusted his hat. "Don't know about heaven. I ain't seen it."

James swallowed a lump. He thought about yanking the wool blanket down but he needed to know more. He wanted to understand the gunslinger. The reason behind his trouble. He tried to stare at the coal black eyes.

"You were lucky last time we met. Do you remember?"

"I remember you missing me a bunch."

The gunslinger's expression revealed his anger. "Trust me. You were lucky."

James shrugged. He tried to remember all the words he wanted to use to distract the gunslinger. His mind was blank. All he could do was react to the evil that stood opposite him.

"Well, you called me here. Against my busy schedule. What can I do for you, James?"

"You can leave this town. Now. And never come back."

The gunslinger smiled again. "Not gonna happen, James. You see, I got to make things right."

"Make what right?"

"I have to settle a score."

"Seems to me, if you're dead, the score has already been settled." James took a step forward. His courage returned as the conversation continued.

"It's not that simple."

James took another step toward the gunslinger.

"I wouldn't get any closer, son. You're liable to get hurt."

"I'll take my chances."

"I've grown impatient with your wise mouth, boy. You gonna back up your attitude today? Or are you gonna keep running your mouth like a ten cent whore?"

James laughed this time. He found the challenge funny, but it was mostly nervousness.

"I didn't make a joke."

James stopped laughing.

"That's right, kid. I'm in control here." The words were spoken in his mind again. A chill forced him to shiver.

James watched the gunslinger. His fingers wiggled above his shiny six shooters. The black, soulless eyes revealed nothing. James focused on the hands. It was his only chance. The gunslinger's eyes were too dark to show intent. And his wrinkled, skeletal skin was almost expressionless.

The gunslinger pulled the guns from the holsters and aimed at James in a fraction of a second. The bullets screamed at James quicker than a blinking eye. His only defense was to drop to the dirt.

Two shots sailed high. One from each gun.

The gunslinger laughed. The barrels danced in unison as his belly laughter consumed him.

James spit dust from his lips. He lifted his head to the gunslinger. James wondered why the Sheriff had not returned fire. He figured the Sheriff knew it was useless anyway.

"You're a coward, James." The words were in his head.

James stood up and faced the menace. "If I'm such a coward, then why am I still standing here?"

The gunslinger stopped laughing. "You can still be dumb and a coward."

James took a few steps backward and slipped behind the blanket-covered mirror.

"You can't hide from me, James. I know how to find you."

"Let's see if you can find yourself out of this." James shouted as he whipped the wool blanket from the mirror. The reflection of the gunslinger filled the mirror.

CHAPTER 25

The people were everywhere. Carson held on to Sarah's dress as tightly as he could. It wasn't easy though. Because of his height, Carson's face brushed across elbows and knuckles. And a few smelly rumps when his head was leaned too far forward.

Carson wanted to get outside to help James but he didn't know how he could do it without Sarah noticing. He had no choice but to go along for the ride since Sarah was around him every minute of this day.

He was still upset with James. Carson knew James had tried to ditch him again. He had overheard the conversation in the brothel between Sarah and James. Since that point, his anger swung from James to Sarah and back. Although, he appreciated how Sarah stuck up for him against James. So, Carson found it hard to stay mad at her for too long.

The saloon was so quiet Carson wondered why it was like church services. He tried to look around, as best he could, to see if people were praying. But it seemed that folks just kept quiet. Part of him wanted to shout out to break the awkward silence but he was afraid of how everyone would react toward him. Carson knew that folks didn't like him because he was so stupid.

The dirty man next to him glared down into Carson's face. His wrinkled face snarled, revealing a few gaps in his mouth where teeth should be. Carson tucked his face into Sarah's dress and pulled himself tight against her waist. After a few moments, Carson looked over his shoulder at the cranky man who was no longer paying any attention to him. Relieved, Carson loosened his grip on Sarah.

They were stuck in the middle of the crowd and all the bodies pressed together. Carson looked down at his feet. A shiny coin stared up at him from the dirty floor. Excited with his find, Carson bent down and scooped up the lost treasure. He rolled the coin through his fingers, enjoying the sensation. The smoothed edges reminded Carson of the edges of a deck of cards. Rubbing his finger along it soothed him. He suddenly wished he were playing poker with James.

Above Carson, the mob shifted forward a bit and Sarah moved too. He was about to scramble for Sarah's dress when he realized this might be his chance to escape. If he could sneak away, then he could help James. And then all would be forgiven. Carson wouldn't be mad at them if he got to join the adventure.

Carson remained crouched down. He looked up in Sarah's direction but she was cloaked by other people. So Carson half crawled and half duck-walked through the legs and skirts towering over him. His hand clutched the coin while his index finger stroked the smooth edge.

He reached the rear of the saloon within a few minutes. A long blue dress covered the lower portion of the back door. Carson started to crawl under the dress, between the legs of the woman above. He only made it a few inches before the legs clamped shut around his ribs and squeezed. Carson wanted to scream out in defiance of this restraint but he remembered that the room was silent. So he wiggled to the right and bit down on the woman's calf. She raised her leg up off the floor in reaction to the bite. Amazingly, the woman refrained from crying out in pain, even though her boot stomped back down to the floor. In that brief moment, Carson shimmied forward and pushed the back door open with the crown of his head.

Carson crawled a few more steps before turning to watch the saloon door close behind him. The woman in the blue dress scowled at him and shook an angry fist in his direction. Carson grinned and then stuck his tongue out right before the door clicked shut.

The mid-day sun was hot and Carson felt the top of his head heat up. He scratched his dirty blond hair with the coin and then stood up in the alley. Garbage was piled up behind the saloon along with barrels of ale and bourbon. As he stood, Carson noticed how quiet it was outside too. Besides the bustle of the traffic in the street, he usually heard some birds singing or dogs barking. Creatures of all sizes joined the cacophony of life. But not today. An eerie silence draped over the town and it made goosebumps rise on Carson's forearms.

The clock tower chimed.

Carson jumped as the sound startled him back to the present. He looked left and right. Which way should he go? If he went left, he would come into the street behind the gunslinger's spot. If he went right, he would be in front of the gunslinger. And that scared Carson. He squeezed his penis through his pants to stop himself from peeing from the fright of being this close.

Dong!

Carson scrambled to the left and ran through the gap between the buildings. The street was empty in front of him.

Dong!

He slid his back down along the saloon's outer wall and tried to catch his breath.

Dong!

Carson leaned his head slightly around the corner to face the clock tower. James stood in the middle of the street before the clock. Behind him was the mirror covered with a blanket.

Dong!

Carson tucked his head back behind the wall. He started to hyperventilate as the seriousness of this adventure became all too real.

Dong!

A little pee trickled out as Carson's fear rose to a crescendo. He noticed his hands shaking on his knees and he felt like he was going to black out.

Dong!

Carson stroked the edge of the coin and his mind eased a bit. He took a deep breath and thought about all the times he and James had talked about fighting bad guys.

Dong!

He scrambled along the porch boards in front of the saloon.

Dong!

Carson jumped behind a support beam on the saloon's porch. He caught the horrified looks on the faces in the saloon doorway staring at him. Carson clutched the post and leaned to the side to keep his eyes on the action.

Dong!

Now the moment had arrived, he thought. This was his chance to help James and become a hero. Just like James' daddy.

Dong!

His fear abated and he imagined himself punching the gunslinger with his forehead like James did to that bad man in the saloon the other day.

Dong!

CHAPTER 26

James ducked behind the mirror. He glanced around the side to see if the gunslinger had disappeared. The apparition stood motionless with a blank expression upon its face. James was surprised that the mirror hadn't trapped the gunslinger. But it apparently had some sort of effect as the ghost stared motionlessly.

The black eyes never blinked. The wrinkles along its eyes contracted as it squinted at its reflection.

Bang! Bang!

Quicker than a blink, the gunslinger raised his pistols and fired two shots into the looking glass. As the shards tinkled to the dirt below, James covered his head and lowered himself to the earth. Before he could raise his head, James heard the creaky laughter.

"You fool." The gunslinger croaked gravelly.

James looked up as the gunslinger took several steps in his direction. Each time the spurs jingled, James flinched like a child watching fireworks. He panted, each exhale puffing little clouds of dust from the soil.

"A man doesn't lie down when he finds himself in a fight."

James lost his cool and sprang to his feet. He watched the gunslinger closely, while he slowly moved his arm toward his pistol.

"Go ahead, James. Reach for that piece."

James halted. How did the ghost know he was reaching for his gun? Could this thing read his mind? Or did it have the ability to see everything in its surroundings, like some sort of soothsayer? James was befuddled and his mind went blank as to how he should react.

"Choosing to die like a man is admirable."

"I'm not choosing to die."

"What would you call it then? If you chose to live, James, then you wouldn't have been here at all."

The gunslinger had a point, James reasoned. He started to second guess his cockamamie plan and the bravado that led him here. A drop of sweat fell from his brow.

"Now I must make an example of you, James. Like your foolish Mayor. It is one thing to avoid my presence. But it is another to question it. Or mock me." The words oozed out like runny eggs in a skillet. The syllables lingered on the thick air.

"Go ahead, demon. Show the town how tough you are. It must be rewarding to gun down unarmed old men or boys. You must be proud." James taunted the ghost. For the first time in recent memory, James had referred to himself as a boy. He figured, if it helped reinforce his point, he could demean himself temporarily.

"I am not a demon. Nothing possesses my soul…boy." The gunslinger lowered his weapons, placing the six shooters back in his holsters. But he kept his hands hovered above them nonetheless. "Your Mayor may not have been armed with a gun, but he was armed with the knowledge of his involvement."

James screwed up his face. He didn't understand what knowledge had to do with anything. His mind raced to figure out how he could defeat the evil entity. Thoughts of his very survival kept getting in the way. What good could he do if he were dead, he asked himself.

"How about we make a deal?"

"I don't make deals, James."

"There is a first time for everything."

The gunslinger chuckled.

"Maybe there's a way where everyone can win?"

"It's too late for compromise, James. I lost everything. And now I have come back to avenge the wrongs done to me."

James slowly brushed sweat from his forehead with the back of his sleeve. He didn't want to make any sudden movements. Movements that might cause the gunslinger to draw down on him.

"I've learned that it's never too late. For anything."

"Spare me your youthful wisdom, boy. You grow sparse whiskers and yet you preach to me about the ways of the world? You're pathetic."

James' temper flared. His fear evaporated when the apparition called him pathetic.

"You know what's pathetic?" He waited to get a response but none came. "A ghost that picks on innocent people like a bully."

The gunslinger chuckled again. "If you only knew the past, James, you might wonder who was the one being bullied."

James stepped toward the gunslinger. "Well, the way I see it, there's three types of people in this world. Bullies who pick on the weak. People who stand up to the bullies. And cowards."

The black eyes grew darker. The sides of the gunslinger's mouth twitched, making the razor-thin mustache dance upon its upper lip. "What did you say?"

"I'm just wondering which one you are."

"Are you calling me a coward…little boy?"

"You tell me what you are." James stared right into the black eyes. His heart hammered in his chest and he wanted to club this sonofagun in the skull with the handle of his six-shooter. "You say you aren't the bully because someone had bullied you. And you aren't the type to stand up to the bullies. Cause if you did, then you'd probably still be alive. Or, at least, your soul wouldn't come back here for revenge." James looked at his boots and then coyly raised his head back up. "That only leaves one thing, don't it?"

The gunslinger shook and twitched, its bony hands clenched and unclenched with rage. "Do…not…call…me…a coward."

James felt his tongue, dry and stuttering inside his mouth, try to utter the word. He wanted to kick off this fight but some deep recess of his mammalian brain overrode his urges in order to stay alive. The internal struggle waged between his brain and his tongue. Eventually, his tongue would win out.

"Coward."

The gunslinger tipped its head back and hollered at the heavens. The scream was louder than thunder and James heard the windows on the buildings vibrate from the tremors. The ground moved beneath his feet and the sensation traveled from his boots to his chest in seconds.

James reached for his six-shooter. His hands clasped the warm wooden handle. But the barrel caught on his belt loop. James' hand pulled up empty.

The haunted gunslinger ripped his six shooters from their leather holsters as he shrieked. The coal-colored eyes rolled back in their sockets, revealing blacker voids. As the gunslinger leveled the barrels at James, something caught its attention.

"Hey!"

CHAPTER 27

Sheriff Axl Morgan tasted the bile in his mouth. It left an alkaline tang behind, as he swallowed it down. The sun radiated above making his shirt and hands sticky with sweat. He swabbed his brow with a shoulder. Then he lowered the brim of his hat to shade his eyes.

The clock tower chimed, beginning the signal of the noon hour. Each ring caused the hairs on the back of his neck to stand out further. A chill shimmied down his spine and he felt a cold sweat break out on his forearms. It seemed to last for hours but the chiming ended in seconds.

He watched below as the gunslinger came to life down the street. The Sheriff was astonished that James had been able to conjure it up. He had his doubts about this plan from the get-go.

James and the ghost looked smaller than he anticipated. But Sheriff Morgan was confident in his shooting accuracy. He'd taken down deer at a greater distance so this stand shouldn't be difficult. Of course, it still remained to be seen if bullets would have any effect on the gunslinger. They had none last time.

The Sheriff lined the gunslinger up in the iron sights of his rifle. It was a Winchester lever action. The Sheriff had cocked the lever before the gunslinger arrived to avoid the loud clicking noise of feeding a round into the chamber. It also served for a quicker shot should it be needed. He had only half kidded with James that his backup protection could put James out of his misery. Sheriff Morgan whispered a prayer to God above that he wouldn't have to shoot James dead.

He strained like hell to hear what was being said. The voices were muffled by the distance. And, at times, it sounded like James was answering the gunslinger without the apparition saying anything. Why should any of this make sense, the Sheriff thought.

In all his years, Sheriff Morgan never imagined he would be cleaning his town of evil spirits. These types of things were fantastic lore for campfires or sermon parables. Yet, here he was. Seeing was definitely believing, in his mind.

James and the gunslinger pointed at each other as they spoke. Several times, they each took steps toward one another. If James survived this, the Sheriff planned on bottling whatever filled that boy's kiwis. Folks would line up for miles to get their hands on such courage.

As he took his eye off the iron sights, Sheriff Morgan witnessed James spring into action. He jumped behind the mirror and, with one slick motion, tugged off the blanket. The gunslinger appeared to freeze before firing several rounds at James. The mirror shattered into millions of fragments. James was laid out on the ground and the Sheriff believed James had been shot.

He lined up the iron sights again with his left eye closed. Movement caught his eye and he saw that James got back up and stood before the broken mirror. He strained to hear what was being said but he was only able to pick up a few words here and there. It was enough to follow along, in general. James was taunting the gunslinger. Damn you, James. The Sheriff screamed at the kid in his head, while he re-focused the gun on the ghost.

He swung the barrel back and forth between the gunslinger and James. It was better to be prepared for a kill shot on either of them depending on how events turned out. From this distance, he only had to move the barrel of the gun a few inches to cover the expanse. The Sheriff took a deep breath and held it to steady his hands.

Suddenly, the gunslinger started screaming. The volume of the screams was deafening. Sheriff Morgan felt the shrieks vibrate through his body before he actually heard them. James reached behind his back for his firearm. But for some reason his hand was empty. The gunslinger drew both pistols and aimed at James. The moment was fleeting. Yet, the Sheriff thought it had been an eternity.

Just as the gunslinger prepared to fire his guns at James, a voice shouted down below. The Sheriff exhaled his breath with surprise. Apparently, the gunslinger had been just as surprised. It froze in place and turned to face the newcomer. Sheriff Morgan leaned as far as he could without falling off the roof of the general store. Whoever had interrupted the fight managed to remain out of his sight lines.

He shot a glance back at the gunslinger and noticed the cold, black eyes. They appeared cavernous and filled with darkness. A darkness that made hell look like a civilized resort. Then he saw James. James wore a terrified expression and his eyes grew wide with fear.

Just then, several gunshots sounded. Each bang made the Sheriff's eyelids clap shut. He lost count of how many shots were fired. A puff of gray smoke emanated from each six shooter in the hands of the gunslinger.

His heart sank as he realized where those shots were aimed. He had no doubts that death had come calling, once again. His mind's eye flashed images of blood flowing like rivers. Splatter along the wooden porch boards. Dead eyes staring beyond the sun. And flies crawling into lifeless mouths and nostrils.

It happened so fast. As much as they had prepared for this showdown, the Sheriff and James were not prepared for the carnage that swept through town.

Somewhere high above, a hawk circled along the currents. Its beady eyes made plans for supper. It screeched aloud to invite its friends over for their next meal.

CHAPTER 28

Sarah felt uncomfortable. An eerie sensation overtook her and she suddenly couldn't stand still. It made her nervous. Sarah couldn't explain the feeling but it was so pervasive.

Something felt ominous and Carson's face flashed before her eyes. The clock tower chimed.

Sarah mouthed "Excuse me" without uttering a sound to the faces that stood behind her. Eyes rolled, women tsked and subtle huffs erupted quietly as she fought to make her way toward the back of the bar. Of course, a few brazen men took the opportunity to elbow her or worse, fondle her lady parts, as she made her way. She ignored the physical assaults because Carson's safety was far more important. She did take the time to make mental notes of faces though so she could exact retribution at a later point in time.

She admonished herself for being so careless with him. Carson was old enough to take care of himself but his capabilities were less adequate. A youngster with his state of mind could get himself hurt or killed. He just didn't understand everything that occurred around him. And that filter that warned a person when something wasn't right or maybe danger was close by...well, it didn't always signal like it would for a regular person. Sarah wanted to scream out loud at herself for being so foolish.

Dong!

It suddenly dawned on her that Carson had mentioned his frustration with James leaving him behind on these "adventures". Could he have gone off to join James? No, that's absurd. He knew where James and Sarah stood on the idea. She panicked with these thoughts. It would be just like a little boy to go and do what he wasn't supposed to. Memories of James as a child played before her.

She squeezed and pushed a little more forcefully. Her compulsion to find Carson gave her an extra boost of energy. She stopped and ducked down every few steps. As she neared the back door to the saloon, a woman with a blue dress shot her a dirty look. Sarah wanted to just stick her head out the door to see if Carson was playing in the alley. She silently mouthed "Excuse me" to the woman. But the woman shook her head back and forth. Sarah was shocked at the response.

Dong!

She leaned in close to the woman's ear and whispered as quietly as she could. "Please, I just want to peek outside for a moment."

The woman shook her head again and leaned into Sarah's ear. "I already got pushed around by a snot-nosed little boy and I'm not about to get pushed again."

Sarah stared at the lady. "A little boy pushed you? What did he look like?"

Dong!

The woman whispered back. "Sandy messy hair. Brown eyes and a tan shirt."

Sarah's eyes widened. "That's my son. Where did he go?" She held the woman's shoulders tight as she whispered. The woman's face took on a scared countenance from Sarah's tight grip. She nodded her head over her shoulder toward the alley. Sarah shoved the woman to the side, knocking into a wall of people, who all turned with angry eyes.

Dong!

She opened the door and stepped out into the alley. Sarah's eyes scanned the heaps of trash. She didn't find Carson. Sarah almost shouted out his name but caught herself from making noise. She found it increasingly more difficult to breathe. Her chest spasmed as it tried to keep up with her pounding heart.

Dong!

She started to go left and reached the end of the building. Sarah saw James across the street. He stood before the mirror as the noon hour struck.

Dong!

She didn't see Carson on this side of the building so she turned and ran back through the alley.

Dong!

Sarah turned the far corner of the building. Her heart skipped a beat. This side of the building was empty too.

Dong!

Where could he be? Did he go upstairs to their room? He couldn't have done that because he would have taken the stairs from inside the saloon. She screamed in her head for answers. A pit in her stomach formed. Could he have gone out front? If he was still hell-bent on helping James, where else would he have gone? She worried in her head over the possibility.

Dong!

Sarah sprinted in the rocky soil to the front corner of the saloon. From this vantage, she could still see James poised before the mirror. A crackling, static noise reverberated in the center of town. As the last chime sounded, a murky vision of the gunslinger came to life. Sarah's stomach sank.

It was here. James had done it. He had figured out how to summon the ghost. She lost herself in thoughts centered on James and his safety. She forgot about Carson for a moment. Sarah started to say a prayer in her mind that James would not get hurt…or worse. Her eyes teared up as his youth scrolled in front of her eyes.

All of a sudden, Sarah caught movement out of the corner of her right eye. She turned to see what moved down the porch boards.

It was Carson!

He stood behind a support beam as he peeked around the side of the wood.

Sarah almost screamed out loud. Her hand shot up to her mouth to halt her words. The tears flowed as she stood to lose both boys. James stood before the gunslinger. And Carson was too close for comfort.

Sarah's lips quivered as she repeated her prayers. This time for both of them.

CHAPTER 29

The gunslinger appeared and Carson trembled once again. His momentary courage subsided and he wished he had not come outside. Carson rested his head against the post, while his fingernails dug into the wood. He found it difficult to breathe and his chest began pounding.

The boogiedman isn't real. The boogiedman isn't real. The boogiedman isn't real. He repeated the thoughts in his head to calm his fears. It was a little trick his mother had taught him when he was younger. Carson used to wet the bed because he was too scared to use the bed pan in the middle of the night. His mind filled with images of green squishy things and long arms with claws. Those monsters would be waiting for him under the bed or in the corner. But his mommy told him to just close his eyes tight and repeat that the monsters weren't there. It had helped him on some occasions. Not on others.

Carson sucked in some hot air and tilted his head around the beam. He slowly opened his left eye to peek at the gunslinger. Yup. It was there; he shivered. His head retracted behind the post.

He thought he caught an almost inaudible whisper coming from behind him. He was too scared to turn and look though. Carson figured it was one of the faces in the saloon door trying to get him to run away. He knew he would, if only his legs would work. They felt rooted to the porch, even though they trembled.

The gunslinger and James spoke. Carson listened as best he could with all the thumping in his chest. He wondered why his ears heard what was happening in his heart. A thought flashed in his mind that maybe the gunslinger could hear his heart pounding.

A couple loud bangs forced Carson to jump in place. He peeked around the post and saw that the mirror was broken. All the glass twinkled in the street. Some of the flashes from the shards hurt his eyes. He squinted against the shine.

James was lying on the ground. Carson thought he had been shot. He breathed a sigh of relief when James lifted his head and spoke to the gunslinger. James jumped up and walked a few paces toward the gunslinger. Carson was relieved that James was okay. It also brought his bravery back a little. If James could survive the gunslinger's bullets, then they could beat this ghost.

Carson looked to the right to see if there was a better spot that he could watch the action from. He wanted to get closer to James somehow. His current position was directly to the right of the gunslinger. Carson wanted to be in front of the gunslinger so he could team up with James. Nothing for him to hide behind seemed to be within close proximity. Carson decided to stay put.

His mind wandered to all the times James read newspaper clippings out loud. The stories of Wyatt Earp knocking men out. Chasing thieves and hustlers from town. The boys would daydream about taking over for the living legend. They would do things as a team. Together. The memories flooded back and Carson felt stronger with each passing image.

This was it, he thought. All their dreams were about to come true. They would defeat the haunted gunslinger and send him away. Everyone in town would clap and cheer. There would be a parade through the center of town. And maybe all the cake he could eat. Or cookies. Carson licked his lips as he pictured the spoils of victory.

He had to signal James that he was here to help. Carson looked around for a stone or pebble big enough that he could throw to James. James would then see Carson and they would work together. But Carson didn't find anything, within reach, that fit the bill. His hand stroked the coin he had found. But there was no way he would throw that at James. It was a treasure. And he had found it. Fair and square. Carson shoved the coin in his pocket and peeked around the column again.

James seemed to be teasing the ghost. He kept saying things that got the gunslinger angry. A couple times, James answered the ghost even when the ghost didn't talk. Carson wondered who James was talking to when he did that. It seemed weird that he would talk to someone else when nobody was around. He scratched his head but couldn't figure it out.

He had to make a move. Carson didn't want to sit behind the post and watch. He wanted to hit the ghost. He just needed James to distract it somehow. It was difficult finding the right time since James and the gunslinger kept talking to each other. Carson hoped James would get closer and fight the boogiedman so he could run over and jump in. There was still too much room between the two.

The gunslinger was agitated that James had called him a coward. The tension in the air was so strong Carson felt a shiver run down his legs. He realized he still had to pee really badly.

The ghost started screaming at the sky. The windows and porch boards trembled from the vibration of the screams. Carson felt it shake through his stomach. Something was about to happen. He could feel it. The time to jump in came sooner than he thought. Carson decided he had to act now. If he waited for James and the gunslinger to fist fight, it might be too late.

Suddenly, the gunslinger pulled his guns out and aimed at James. Carson's heart stopped. It couldn't end like this. James couldn't die. He had to stop this right away. It was up to Carson to draw the gunslinger's attention away from James. It would save his best friend's life and it would give him a chance to attack without guns pointed at him.

Carson took a deep breath. He stepped around the support beam and took a few steps into the street. Neither the gunslinger nor James had noticed him yet. The word flew from his mouth before he realized he had spoken.

"Hey!"

The gunslinger turned and shot.

Carson blinked as the bullets flew his way.

CHAPTER 30

The shout had taken the gunslinger by surprise. He had been so focused on James and his insults. It never occurred to him that somebody else was close by.

His immediate reaction was to question the outcry. Who the hell is this kid? What is he doing here? The thoughts dashed through his skull. The rest of the town ran away or hid in the safety of the shadows. But not this boy. Why?

Then he understood. The kid's eyes darted to James. They spoke of a deeper connection to James than words could ever convey. The gunslinger knew instantly which path to take. Like a dog playing with a wild rabbit, the gunslinger focused his energy on the small boy.

Hurting the kid would send shock waves through James' soul. And still give him something to look forward to. The gunslinger knew James would lose his focus as he tried to protect his friend. Sometime in the near future, the gunslinger would return to finish burying the rabbit's bones.

He stole a quick glance at James. His eyes as big as cow patties with realization of what was coming. The gunslinger turned back toward the boy. The small face lost its color. His jaw hung down in terror. The eyes squeezed shut to avoid the oncoming onslaught.

The gunslinger pulled the triggers. He watched one bullet pass through the boy's chest. A spray of crimson splashed the front of the saloon. His body jerked backward, lifting off the porch wood. Another bullet ripped through the boy's hand as it flailed through the position that the body had been in just a second ago. Two more bullets sailed in through the saloon's swinging doors. The gunslinger grinned as he heard those bullets find meat. He just couldn't see the targets in the shadows behind the flapping doors.

James screamed for him to stop shooting but he ignored the request. He stole a glance over his left shoulder as James hurried to the saloon. And his pal. He chuckled to himself that he had predicted James' reaction accurately. The gunslinger licked his rotted lips. He thought of finishing off the boy with a few more rounds plugged into the prone, lifeless body. Then he thought better of it.

The gunslinger wanted to take it up a notch. An abundance of death would certainly reinforce his point for revenge. These people had brought it upon themselves. Maybe not the specific souls he dispatched to the afterlife. But it was a small enough town. The deceased were probably related, on some level, to those who had wronged him in the past. They had taken so much from him. And now he was getting something back.

His spurs jangled as he strode to the saloon doors. The gunslinger parted them with the barrels of the six shooters. Then he opened fire on the mob of people stacked deep. Some folks knelt over the dead and dying, oblivious of his arrival. They would get a pass, he reasoned.

The bullets quickly ran out. He kept pulling the triggers as the cylinders revolved with empty clicks. He had enjoyed himself so much he hadn't realized he needed to reload. The gunslinger re-holstered his guns and snatched six shooters from the dead bodies at his feet. He picked right up where he had left off.

Lead smacked into bone with a slapping sound. Some bullets ran through several torsos before coming to rest in a bloated liver or charred lung. Ripping sounds echoed off the wooden floors as flesh scissored open to expose muscle and sinew. The gunslinger loved the sounds which drowned out the hysterical cries and terrified shrieks. Men became women and women became children as the living clawed their way over each other for safety.

The gunslinger leaned down to the bloody face of a crying woman. He laughed hard, inches from her wide eyes. The smell of blood and other fluids filled his nostrils. He stopped laughing momentarily, to breathe in the sweet scent of death. Then he stood and continued to laugh.

The room was full of chaos. Bloody bodies littered the floor. A writhing pile of injured stacked waist high in the middle of the bar. The gunslinger knew these people had been trampled by the spineless rodents that scrambled for safety. Another lump of people cluttered the back door's port. They were the unlucky ones who were stuffed into the walls as folks fought their way out the back door. Bedlam in every direction. The gunslinger was satisfied with his destruction. He dropped the guns on the bloody floor and turned to leave the saloon, through the swinging doors. He didn't bother to avoid the bodies, choosing to step on whatever lie before him.

As the gunslinger stepped onto the porch, the noises coming from his right grabbed his attention. James was kneeling with the boy's head cradled in his lap. He cried profusely and begged God to save the poor kid. The gunslinger snickered to himself. Good luck, James. There is no God. Trust me.

His eyes followed the woman's hands as she tried to stop the bleeding hole in the boy's chest. He knew, as big as the hole looked on the front, it would be even bigger on the kid's back. Blood soaked the floor boards and he thought to himself that little people sure held a lot of blood inside.

The woman looked up at his vacant eyes. Her long black hair looked crazy as it came apart from the bun on the top. Her crystal-blue eyes were red, and full of tears. She breathed heavily and her stare told him how much hatred she had for the gunslinger. He didn't mind. He didn't come to this town to win friends and settle down. He came here to finish old business. To collect on debts owed.

To fulfill a legacy of revenge.

James' tearful eyes rose to meet the cold blackness of his own. The gunslinger tipped his brim at James.

"Don't worry, James. I'll be back for you." He grinned wide and chuckled. "I haven't forgotten the fact that you called me a coward."

James stared at him as he strolled into the middle of the street. The gunslinger stopped and stared up at the clock tower. Then he faced James again.

"No need to wait for the noon hour anymore. I'm ready whenever you are…kid."

The gunslinger faded into the sunlight, disappearing into the ether.

CHAPTER 31

A makeshift hospital was set up under the eaves of the saloon. Some people were so injured that Sheriff Morgan implored Doc Stinson to go along with his decision. His argument was to get folks immediate medical attention without having to move the injured clear across town. Besides, the Doctor didn't have that much room in his quaint, formal hospital.

Doc Stinson and his two nurses attended to the wounded. Ambulatory patients sat on the porch boards or stacks of grain bags. The more severe patients were laid out on cots that practically touched each other. There were that many and the goal was to keep them in the shade of the eaves.

Sheriff Morgan watched the undertaker. He squatted down with a tape measure, measuring the size of the dead. Every few seconds he called out the numbers while his assistant scratched out the measurements on a small chalkboard. Bereaved family members stood nearby, crying and consoling each other in the midst of the business-like preparation of the undertaker. The Sheriff shook his head with disgust.

He glanced at James and Sarah, who held hands next to Carson. The little boy was placed on a cot since his injuries were pretty bad.

James moved the cot off to the corner of the saloon, which was in the shade of the building but not under the eaves. Sheriff Morgan approached them with reverence. He couldn't believe Carson had been one of the casualties.

The Sheriff had scrambled down from the roof of the general store when the gunslinger shot up things. He hadn't bothered to shoot the specter for two reasons. First, his instinct pulled him to the aid of the townspeople who were injured. Second, he had never really believed his shot would harm the ghost. He'd seen it with his own eyes when the Mayor died. He spotted James from the roof more for moral support and to save James from suffering. He knew it was morbid, but the Sheriff knew the truth of the west. And it wasn't pretty at times.

"James. Sarah. How is he doing?" The Sheriff removed his hat to greet them.

James looked up with swollen eyes. Streaks of tears lined his cheeks but he wasn't crying at the moment.

"Doc says he's stable. For now."

Sheriff Morgan nodded. "Pretty lucky little fella, I'd say."

"Yeah. At least the bullet missed his lung. But Doc thinks he'll be bandaged up for a while. Not much use of his arm or shoulder."

"Could be worse."

James nodded and looked down at Carson. Sarah dabbed the boy's forehead with a damp rag. She seemed to be whispering prayers as she tended to the boy. Sarah didn't look up at the Sheriff. All her attention was on Carson. The Sheriff nodded his head to request James step aside for a chat. James patted Sarah's shoulder and then followed the Sheriff to the other side of the alley.

"Plan didn't work too well."

James looked down.

"We can't allow this to happen again. We have to do something."

"I know."

"What should we do next?"

"I don't know." James took his hat off and scratched his messy hair. "But we can't do anything here. Too many people around. It's gotten too dangerous."

"Agreed."

James put his hat back on his head. "I don't understand what his beef is. Why does he keep coming back for revenge? Who is he? What happened?" He showed his frustration by waving his hands around with each question.

Sheriff Morgan bit the inside of his cheek. He couldn't hide the truth anymore. "James, every town has its history. A story, if you will."

James stared at the Sheriff.

"Sometimes these stories are happy. Other times, they ain't."

"What are you trying to say, Sheriff?"

The Sheriff looked at the clock tower and then back at James. "This town has some ghosts."

"I know. We just saw what it did to Carson. And those people." James pointed at the row of bodies.

"Not those kinds of ghosts. The kind that linger in our hearts. Our souls."

"Sheriff, what the hell are you driving at?"

"I know who the gunslinger is. And I know why he is here."

"You know?" James appeared agitated. His face contorted with anger.

"We all know. This town knows. I guess it's time that you know too."

James shoved the Sheriff in the chest. Hard. Sheriff Morgan grabbed James by the shirt and cocked his fist as if to strike. But he got himself quickly under control. "Don't touch me, James. Don't…ever…touch me like that."

"You knew? And you didn't think to fill me in? Why?"

"This town…these people, swore to each other the ghosts of the past would remain buried. Unspoken."

"I'll tell you what is going to be buried, Sheriff."

"Keep your voice down."

"Why should I? If everyone knows what's going on, there is no need to keep it quiet, right?"

"It's not a matter of keeping things quiet, James. It's a matter of letting these people tend to their wounds peacefully."

"What about our wounds? Carson's wounds?"

The Sheriff exhaled with his hands out before him. "Look, you have every reason to be upset. But screaming at each other isn't going to solve anything. We need to work together to rid this problem."

"I thought we WERE working together. But I made a mistake. I thought you were trying to help me but you weren't. You were just using me."

James stormed back to Carson's side. He sat down and rubbed Sarah's shoulders as she tended to the little boy.

Sheriff Morgan rubbed his graying beard. He knew he was wrong for hiding the truth from James. He should have been honest from the beginning. He had hoped they could solve the problem without digging up the old bones of the past. The secrets of the past were still too fresh. Too sensitive. The Sheriff hated himself for his involvement in the mystery.

He'd have to let James cool off and then maybe he could talk to him later. For now, he would have to see about getting the dead off the streets and repairing the damage to the town. The psychic damage more than the physical.

CHAPTER 32

It had been a long day. Longer than James cared for. He had failed to defeat the gunslinger. Carson had gotten hurt. People had died. The town was in mourning. And everyone had lied to James. Even Sheriff Morgan.

He kicked off his boots and massaged his sore feet. His stomach growled with hunger. Breakfast was the last meal he had eaten. If he weren't so exhausted, he would bother to feed himself. James wondered when his mother would come home. She had chosen to stay with Carson a while longer.

James reclined on his bed and stared at the ceiling. His body felt like it was melting into the threadbare mattress. Tonight, the old bedding seemed like a fluffy, thick cloud.

His mind replayed the day's events. He tried to figure out what he could have done differently. No matter how he sized it up, the one piece he couldn't control was Carson. The only thing he could have done better was to beat the gunslinger quicker. Then maybe Carson wouldn't have found time to get in the way. Of course, he thought, if the mirror had worked, everything else wouldn't have happened.

He rubbed his eyes. Visions of Carson plagued him. It had all happened so fast, but, in his head, the scene progressed slowly so every minute detail became vivid. James tried to speed along the parts where blood spurted from Carson. It didn't work though. He felt like crying but he was too tired for tears too.

James thought about how his bad decisions would haunt him more than any ghost ever could. He now had to face the townspeople with his failures and mistakes. Worse, how could he ever get Carson to trust him again? He had lied to Carson and left him behind. Multiple times now. And, to top it off, Carson had gotten shot. Not once, but twice. How much bad luck could one little boy take? James sighed.

A knock at the door shook James from his thoughts. He was glad for the distraction since time alone meant time to live with his demons. His body didn't exactly cooperate with him though. It seemed content to stay put. He willed himself to shuffle to the door as the knocks became louder and more frequent.

James opened the door. He stared at the visitor with a surprised expression.

"Hello, James."

"Eleanor."

"I'm sorry to stop by this late and unannounced. May I speak with you?"

James' initial reaction was delight. It quickly soured as he remembered the Sheriff's admission that the whole town was in on the story. He grimaced and waved his hand to invite her in. Eleanor smiled and brushed past James. He got a dizzying whiff of her fragrance as she went by.

Eleanor looked around for a place to sit. James didn't want her to stay long so he didn't offer her a seat. "What do you want?"

"I heard about today. I had chosen to leave town for safety's sake. Everyone is talking about it. I'm sorry things didn't go the way you wanted."

"It might have gone better if I had known the truth."

Eleanor tilted her head. "Truth? What truth?"

"Don't play games with me. I know there is some kind of secret around here about the gunslinger."

James noticed the shock on her face. He got angrier that she was going to keep up the ruse.

"I don't know what that means."

"You can stop pretending now. You're only making me madder and I don't like being lied to." He took a few steps toward her with his hands clenched.

"James, I am not lying to you. I really have no idea what you are talking about." She had her hand on her chest as if she were offended by his claims.

He tried to size her up. Could she be telling the truth, he wondered? Before he could figure it out, Eleanor continued.

"How is Carson?"

"Doc Stinson says he'll live. The bullet passed through without hitting any organs. But he lost a lot of blood. So…"

"Poor thing. I hope he has a speedy recovery."

"Me too."

An awkward silence filled the air as they both looked around the room for relief.

"Well, I guess I should be going then." Eleanor walked to the door. James didn't follow her. Instead, he asked a question with his back still to her.

"Why did you REALLY come here tonight?" He turned toward her.

Eleanor still faced the door with her hand on the knob. James thought she was frozen in place because she wasn't moving and she paused for several moments before answering.

"I…wanted to make sure you were okay."

"Then I guess you got what you came for."

She nodded and reached for the door.

"Eleanor."

She turned to face James. He thought her eyes were watered but it was hard to tell in the dim lighting.

"You really know nothing about the gunslinger?"

"No."

"Cause Sheriff Morgan told me that everyone in town has known the secret for years."

"Secret? What secret?"

"I don't know. Yet. But I'm fixin' to find out."

Eleanor looked at her hands. "I only came to town ten months ago."

James was shocked. If she had come to town that recently, she wasn't even here the last time the gunslinger showed up. He felt foolish now for treating Eleanor so poorly. But how could he fix it, he wondered. James just nodded.

"Well, goodnight." Eleanor reached for the door again.

"Goodnight." James stayed in place.

As Eleanor opened the door to leave, Sarah was about to come in.

"Oh. Ms. Johnson. Good evening." Eleanor stammered with surprise.

Sarah appeared just as surprised. She rested her hands on her hips.

"Miss Lark." She stepped across the threshold and stood nose to nose with Eleanor. "What are you doing here? At night? With James?" Her eyes darted from Eleanor to James and back.

"She was just leaving, Mother."

Sarah brushed past Eleanor to approach James. "That doesn't answer my question. Does it?"

James looked down at his feet with embarrassment. Did she really think that they were up to no good in light of the day's events? He showed his frustration. "She just stopped by to make sure I was alright."

"Isn't that thoughtful?" Sarah's tone was very sarcastic. She spun around, shoved Eleanor through the door and slammed it shut behind her.

CHAPTER 33

"I want the truth, right now." James slammed the door and stomped over to the desk. Sheriff Morgan looked up at him under the brim of his hat.

"Good morning, James. Why don't you come in?" The Sheriff was sarcastic.

"If I'm gonna beat this ghost, I need to know what happened. All of it." James slammed his fist on the desk. He tried to hide how much the hard wood hurt his hand.

"Sit down, James." The Sheriff removed his hat and settled back in his chair. "I owe you. You're right."

The admission took some of the fire out of James' hostility. He sat in the hard chair before the large desk. James was still wary about whether the Sheriff would truly come clean.

The Sheriff lit a cigarette. He offered James one but James shook it off. He had never smoked before and he wasn't about to start now. James had always hated the smell, as it choked his lungs.

"Several years back, this town went through some…growing pains." He blew smoke toward the ceiling. "The Mayor and some friends of his took things a bit too far."

James shifted in the chair. "How so?"

"Well, let's start by acknowledging what the Mayor did to build this great town. In the beginning, folks just showed up and staked claims to land. Started building what they wanted, wherever they wanted. It got pretty crazy." He took another drag of the cigarette, held the smoke and then exhaled the plumes through his nostrils.

"Mayor Samuels took control. He knew how to talk to folks. Got them together, agreeing on things they didn't even want just minutes before he had dealt with them. But he did it because he loved the town. The idea of the town. He had a vision, unlike everybody else."

James stared at the Sheriff. He absorbed the tale with great interest. James was never one for learning but he had to admit this historical perspective was interesting.

"Anyhow, these friends of Samuels were interested in a parcel a few miles from here, by the creek. But the land was already settled by this farmer. Dodson. Francis Dodson. Went by the name Doddy."

James settled back in the chair. He got goosebumps thinking about how fascinating this story was.

"So these friends paid Doddy a visit. He wasn't interested in their offers for him to vacate. This went back and forth a few times until Doddy chased them off with some buckshot. The friends demanded Samuels help them out so he tried to share his vision with Doddy too. Doddy would have none of it. So the Mayor came back with his tail between his legs. And his friends weren't happy. They demanded he legislate the land to them but he refused. Told them it wasn't right to take just for takings sake." The Sheriff paused to crush out his butt on the floor. James leaned forward with impatience.

"And?"

"And the friends waited for Doddy to work his fields. While he was out, they burned the place to the ground. Problem was, Doddy's wife, Martha, and his six-year old daughter, Sally, were in the house. They burned up with the home."

James dabbed sweat from his upper lip. "That's awful."

"Yep. Doddy got the message and then brought one of his own. He rode into town, killed two of the Mayor's friends. Then he stormed towards the Mayor's office to finish him off, too."

"Well, he obviously didn't kill the Mayor. At least not back then. So what happened next?"

"I killed him." The words sounded so final. The sentence hung in the air. Palpable, as James swallowed a lump in his throat.

Sheriff Axl Morgan stared off through the window. He rubbed his graying beard. James detected sorrow in the Sheriff's expression.

"So the revenge the gunslinger is after is for what happened to his family?"

"I reckon it is."

"Why is everyone covering it up? Pretending it never happened?"

The Sheriff turned in his chair to face James. "It is the one blemish on this town's record. Plus, folks didn't want to think about the horrible things their own fathers and brothers did to the Dodson family. Guilt by association, I figure."

"And you were left to clean up the Mayor's mess?"

"It wasn't the Mayor's mess. Samuels was against the ploy from the start. They were his friends, sure. But he had nothing to do with the heinous acts. He regretted it for the rest of his life."

James couldn't believe this beautiful town had such a sordid past. He began to wonder which of the citizens he had served in the general store had relatives that had been involved.

"Which families did this to the Dodsons?"

"I'm not going to point out the evil-doers. Enough blood has been spilled already. Besides, I know for a fact the survivors struggle to live with their guilty consciences. They bear the burden every day. And they'll have to answer for it in the next life."

James sighed. He wanted to know who had been involved. Although, he figured it was best he didn't know because he would feel obligated to pay them a visit of his own. He felt his blood boiling as he imagined how he would handle the injustices.

"That's it. The whole story. Now you know what happened and why." He pulled a bottle of whiskey from under the desk and clunked it on the surface. "Interested in a snort?"

James shook his head. He still felt speechless about the town's dark history.

"Well, I need one now."

James got up and circled behind the chair. He scratched his head and watched the Sheriff guzzle two big gulps straight from the bottle. It looked like the Sheriff struggled with the memory. James wasn't sure if it was because of his own hand in ending Doddy's life.

"Can I ask you one more thing?"

"Shoot." The Sheriff whispered through the burn of the alcohol.

"Why noon? Why the shootout?"

Sheriff Morgan leaned his elbows on the desk. "That's how it went down."

James raised his eyebrows in confusion.

"I stopped Doddy on his way to the Mayor's office. He told me to step aside or he would add me to the list. I refused, so he challenged me to a shootout. Said, if he won, he would hunt Samuels down unfettered. And, if he lost… he wouldn't have to live with the loss of his family anymore."

James listened closely.

"I had to do what I had to do. We were supposed to shoot at high noon. But I shot first. On the eleventh chime."

"You what?"

"I was scared, James. I knew he would kill me. So I killed him first."

CHAPTER 34

James ran over to Doc Stinson's. He was excited to see Carson. After meeting with Sheriff Morgan, his mother told him Carson had regained consciousness. Apparently, Carson opened his eyes and asked for James. Sarah wasted little time coming home to inform James.

He swung open the door and trotted to the back of the office. Makeshift cots had been set up in between the standard hospital beds. The patient room was chaotic with the injured and their visiting loved ones. James worked his way toward the rear where Carson lie.

James approached the bed and saw that Carson's eyes were closed. He looked over the heavy bandage covering Carson's right arm and shoulder. The bandage wound around his neck, down his right side and ended in a puffy ball on his right hand. A dried circle of blood stood out in the center of the bandage on his hand.

"James?"

Carson's eyes fluttered open and he appeared to be happy to see James.

"Hey buddy. How are you feeling?"

Carson tried to shrug but the pain on his right side caused him to wince. Instead, he spoke. "Fine."

James sat on the bed and rubbed Carson's leg. "We've missed you around here."

"Did you kill the boogiedman?"

"Bogeyman, not boogiedman. No. He got away again."

"You left me again."

James looked away. He felt uncomfortable facing the disappointment he had caused. "I know, buddy. But I didn't want you to get hurt." As soon as he said it, James rolled his eyes as he realized Carson actually had gotten very hurt.

"You lied to me, James. You lied." Carson's eyes filled with tears. He rolled his head away from James. It made it easier for him to speak with Carson but it also kicked in some extra guilt.

"Carson...I don't know what I would do if you got badly hurt. Or worse. I didn't want to put you in a situation that was too dangerous."

"But we are supposed to be a team. You said so. All those times in our hiding spot. You said we would fight bad guys together." Carson's voice had gotten louder and folks started to look their way. James smiled at them as they shot him dirty looks. He turned back to Carson.

"I know. I did say those things. And I meant it..."

"Then why? Why did you lie?"

Each time Carson accused James of lying, his heart broke. He knew Carson was devastated by his betrayal. But how could he reason with a boy? A boy who struggled to understand the world, no less? James was at his wit's end trying to figure out how to gently let down Carson.

"Mommy said you were my friend. Like a brother. And you are supposed to take care of me while she is away. I'm going to tell her what you did, when she comes home." Carson whimpered his threat.

James put his head in his hands. He hadn't even remembered the lie about Carson's mother. In a flash, James realized that he had lied to this sweet kid too many times. He hated himself for it, even if it had all been out of love. How could he continue to look Carson in the face? Coming clean on one lie wasn't coming clean enough. Could he risk letting Carson know what had really happened to his mother? Would he understand? What if telling him about his mother caused him to get sicker, and not heal properly? Would he ever love James again? He bit the side of his hand as he looked into Carson's hurt eyes.

Carson stared at him. James waged an internal battle over his allegiance to his pal and his quest to do what was right. It occurred to James that doing what was right wasn't always the best thing. Look at the situation he found himself in now. He had lied to Carson to protect him and shield him from the harsh realities of the world. And, in doing so, he had damaged the boy's feelings terribly.

"Your mother is dead…Carson." It was out before he could stop it.

Carson stared at James as a huge tear ran down his pale cheek. He didn't say a word. Just stared.

"Crouching Bear killed your mother. Accidentally. That's why I went after him. Without you."

"James." It was more whisper than anything.

"I'm sorry. I…didn't want you to get hurt. So I kept the truth from you. I guess I have told you lots of lies." James couldn't look at Carson. He focused on a snagged stitch on the blanket covering his little friend.

Carson cried hard. He turned his face away from James and cried very hard. People were staring in their direction and James just returned their gaze, without a smile this time. A few people shook their heads in disgust. He played with the snag and kept his head down. He didn't know what else to say. And he wanted to comfort Carson, but what could he possibly say now?

James put his hand on Carson's left shoulder. As soon as Carson felt it, he reacted violently.

"Get out! Get out! I never want to see you again!"

James jumped back, startled. The whole room went silent as everyone paused to watch the scene. James' eyes brimmed with tears.

"Sor…sorry."

"GET OUT! GET OUT! GO AWAY!" Carson's cries grew more hysterical.

A nurse ran over and grabbed James by the elbow. She was trying to pull him away but he fought it off.

"Carson. I'm so sorry."

"You better leave. Now." The nurse grabbed James' elbow with both hands this time. She shoved him away from the bed. As he walked across the room, he heard Carson's wails. They cut through his heart. He cried, too, as he left the room.

The nurse closed the door behind James. She didn't say anything more to him. She didn't need to. James felt awful and he knew he wasn't welcome in the hospital. Especially by Carson.

James sat down on the porch and put his hat on his head. He pulled the brim down low to hide his face. He knew, if anyone walked by, they would be able to figure out he was crying. Through blurry eyes, he watched each large drop land on his dusty boots below.

CHAPTER 35

Sarah was talking with a few of the girls in the parlor when James came home. His expression betrayed a deep sadness, which frightened her. She knew he had gone to see Carson and her heart sank as she thought maybe he had taken a turn for the worse. She excused herself and hustled to catch up with James.

"James? Is everything okay?" She tried to look into his face but he kept his head down.

"Uh-huh." He kept walking down the hall toward their room. James had his hands stuffed into his pockets. His feet shuffled slowly as if he were dragging a cart of boulders behind him.

James reached the door and opened it. He slumped down on his bed and pushed the brim of his hat over his face. Sarah knew something was wrong. James was always so full of life and excitement. It had been a long time since she had seen him this down.

"James, is Carson okay?"

"Yeah."

Sarah felt the relief wash over her. At least Carson's situation hadn't worsened. She bet herself that Miss Lark had something to do with it. If she had done anything to hurt James, she would teach that little lady a thing or two.

"Alright, buster. Spill it."

"I don't feel like talking, Mom."

"I'm sorry. Did I say treat me like rubbish, my King?" Sarah laid the sarcasm on thick. Guilt and sarcasm were her tools of the motherhood trade.

James sighed and lifted the hat to glare at her. He sat up and rested his head in his hands.

Sarah sat down next to him. She rubbed his back gently. When he was a young boy, she would stroke his back to make him feel better after falling down or getting teased by the other children.

"Carson hates me."

"No, he doesn't. Why would you say that?"

"He told me to leave and he never wants to see me again."

Sarah made a face of disbelief. "Oh, why would he say that? He loves you. Your name was the first thing he said when he woke up."

"I told him about his mother."

Sarah shot up off the bed. "You what? Why would you do that? And in his fragile state? That's how you greet him?"

"I can't do it anymore, dang-it."

"Watch your mouth, young man. You may be old enough to make your own decisions but you still need to be respectful around me. I'm your mother."

"Sorry, Mom."

"Now, why would you go and tell him about her? Sometimes you are as thick-headed as your father." She wagged a finger in his face.

"I can't lie to him anymore. I've lied so many times to Carson and all it does is hurt him."

Sarah sighed and sat next to James again. "Oh, honey. Lying to protect him isn't a bad thing."

"Tell him that. You should have seen his face when he called me out on it. I feel terrible."

Sarah understood what he meant. She knew James only had the best of intentions when it came to Carson. She also knew that Carson had trouble understanding the world around him. Even if you explained things to him, he still didn't always follow along.

"How can I leave now with him all sore at me? I can't think about anything but making it right with him."

"He'll come around. He loves you more than anything." She pursed her lips. "So how did he take the news about Minnie?"

James laid back down. He stared at the ceiling. "Well, he cried his eyes out. Then he yelled at me some more for hiding it."

Sarah got up and went to the stove. She placed the tea kettle on it and struck a match to light the fire.

"I'll talk to him. He'll be okay. He's just going to need some extra comforting. And do you know who the queen of comforting is?"

James just pointed at her from his prone position. She chuckled at his boyish gesture. He'll always be a boy, she reminded herself.

"You need to get your head on right before you go off to fight this thing. You've got a job to do. And I don't want you coming back to town feet first." She tried to be comical but it was a mask for her fears. Sarah was trying so hard to let James be grown up and make his own mistakes. But he kept choosing the most dangerous situations to test his luck with. She was extremely anxious about him leaving town. The small consolation was that the Sheriff was accompanying him.

James sat up and wandered to the table. He plopped down on the hard chair and watched Sarah prepare the tea. As she poured two cups, she wished it were whiskey instead.

"A lot of folks are counting on you, James. You made a promise and now you have to see it through." She sipped her tea very quickly to avoid burning her tongue. "I'm counting on you, too. So is Carson."

James looked as if he didn't believe her. She thought for a moment and then tried another tack.

"What's that phrase that Carson always says?"

"You didn't pay attention."

"No, that's not it. Something else."

James looked out the window. Then he repeated Carson's famous line.

"Back to square one."

"That's it. Back to square one." She sipped her tea and watched James. His face brightened a little. She didn't know if he got the message or if he were remembering his little buddy and all the good times they had shared together.

"Well, I reckon I better get back to work on getting ready. I gotta kill this gunslinger and save this town." He brushed his hands on his dungarees.

"Yeah, you do that. Meanwhile, I'll see if I can clean up your messes around here." She grinned at him. James smiled. It was good to see him act more like himself again. What would he do without his momma to take care of him, she thought?

"Thanks, Mom." He bent and kissed her cheek. She slapped his rear and went back to sipping tea. James got busy stuffing some items in his bag.

CHAPTER 36

The men rode in silence at first. James' thoughts were still lingering on Carson and how he had hurt the boy. He figured the Sheriff had been busy replaying the events of the original shootout and the circumstances that led up to it. Either way, they both seemed preoccupied with their thoughts.

"Not sure what we'll find out there. It's been awhile since I've seen it."

James glanced over at the Sheriff. He didn't respond as he searched the horizon. The afternoon sun was waning and it would be dark in a few hours. James hoped they would get there soon so they had some time to look around and set up before nightfall.

"How much longer?"

"Not far now. Just a bit further." The Sheriff rubbed his horse's neck. "I'm still surprised your mother let you come."

James shot the Sheriff a dirty look. "Why wouldn't she let me come? I'm a man, aren't I?"

Sheriff Morgan laughed. "I didn't mean that she gave you permission. I mean just from the standpoint of what we are up against. And she nearly lost your brother." James looked away when he remembered how they had lied about Carson's relationship to them. Where did the lies end, he chided himself.

"If I were her, I would have locked you up and not let you out of my sight."

James smiled. "I had no idea you thought about me that way, Sheriff."

Sheriff Morgan just smirked at James' ribbing as they rode on.

James' face darkened. He thought about the sad tale of the farmer, Doddy, and how he was only trying to do right by his family. He felt sorry for the man and what he had gone through. It still didn't excuse his spirit haunting the townspeople. But James realized the ghost was just a vengeful remainder of a family man. He started to wonder if Crouching Bear's spirit would come back from the dead some day. Then his mind shifted to Carson. James pictured Carson's ghost coming back for revenge against him for lying and casting him aside. He shook the images away as fast as he could.

"Something on your mind, son?"

"Uh, no. Not really."

"You sure, cause you look like you swallowed a big serving of Castor oil after eating a tub of lard."

The imagery turned James' stomach. He choked back some vomit and then tried to change the topic to free his mind. "How long has Miss Lark been in town?" He blushed as soon as the question shot out. He was embarrassed to reveal his feelings for her and of all the things he could have chosen to change the topic, this is what blurts out?

Sheriff Morgan glanced at James. "I reckon about a year ago. Maybe less." His eyes followed the trail. "Why do you ask?"

James shrugged. "She said she wasn't around last time the gunslinger came to town. And she didn't know about Doddy and the farm."

"I told you. Folks don't talk about it. Nobody wants to hang their soiled knickers on the line."

"Still would have helped to know that story before I went up against him."

"How's that? You find any ghost-dropping bullets in the story?"

James shook his head. Why did everyone have to be so dang sarcastic all the time? Then he apologized quietly to his mother for cussing.

They rode on in silence for a while longer. The shadows stretched across the brush and twisted scary shapes out of lonely shrubs. James felt tired. He hadn't slept much recently with all the stress. He couldn't wait to get off the horse and stretch his legs either.

The trail bent to the right through an overgrown copse of trees. Coming through the other side, James saw a fence line in need of repair and a hollowed out expanse with a heap of rubble in the middle of it.

"This is it." The Sheriff stopped his horse. James followed suit and both riders stared at the remnants of a once manicured little lot. A few posts stood, lonely as they stretched to the sky. A crumpled roof leaned against another post that was splintered into the shape of a fork. The lumber was charred and the black remains appeared darker against the setting sun.

"Spooky."

"Yeah, this is all that's left of Doddy's homestead." The Sheriff shifted in his saddle and then hopped down. "It's a shame that nothing came of this parcel after all the blood was shed. Makes you wonder what it was all for." He began leading his horse by the reins.

James slid off his horse and followed the Sheriff on foot. His eyes tried to absorb the wreckage. It was literally burned to the ground. He imagined the woman and her daughter, screaming against the flames for escape. A chill ran down his spine. He wondered if their ghosts haunted this location due to their sudden deaths.

Sheriff Morgan tied his horse to a section of fence that had not yet fallen into a state of disrepair. He pulled his canteen from the saddle bag and took a long swig of water. James did the same. He started to feel scared. Something in his bones told him to turn back now and run like hell. He didn't understand where the feeling came from but it was strong. James looked behind him at the pile of burnt wood. It's just a bunch of garbage. Nothing to be scared of.

Then he saw the bones. The two skeletons, one was longer than the other, began crawling out of the stacks of charred lumber. Both skeletons wore dresses. Only a few swatches of cloth had color. The rest was blacker than coal and fused with the sinews and flesh still left on the bones. James' eyes grew wide and he took several steps back.

"You okay?"

James looked at the Sheriff and then back at the house. There were no more skeletons. He blinked several times as he wondered what had just happened.

"Yeah…I'm okay."

"Good. Cause it looked like you just saw a ghost." The Sheriff snickered softly as he took another sip of water.

James chuckled nervously as he wiped the sweat from his brow.

CHAPTER 37

Sarah exhaled. She had spent the last half hour explaining to Carson why James had lied and left him behind. Carson kept arguing back that buddies didn't lie to each other. And he was frustrated because they had dreamed of going on adventures together since he was little. She heard the disappointment in his voice. But there were only so many times she could go over the same territory.

Carson stared at her as she ran her fingers through her flowing black hair. She had decided to leave it down today because she had a slight headache. The bun always made her headaches worse, pulling her scalp tight.

"So what do you want to do about this then? How can we make this better with you, Carson?"

"I want to fight the gunslinger."

Sarah laughed out loud. Then she saw the seriousness on Carson's face. Could he be serious? Now how do I dance around this one, she thought.

"What?"

"I want to fight the gunslinger."

"Sweetie, you are in no condition to leave this bed, let alone fight a ghostly apparition. That's just silly."

"I'm not silly. I want to go with James."

Sarah almost rolled her eyes but caught herself. She didn't want to get Carson more upset. But she was running out of patience. And she was stumped for how to talk herself out of this one. The boy had been through so much, and if she could just make him happy somehow…

"And what would you do, if you were to magically get out of bed and find yourself by James' side? Hm?"

"I would help him defeat the boogiedman. I would punch him with my head like James done."

Sarah brought her hand to her mouth. She covered up a tiny giggle. Carson was so cute when he mispronounced things. Sarah couldn't help herself sometimes. She just wanted to pinch his cheeks and squeeze him for being so cute.

"Honey, it's a ghost. If you hit it, your head would go right through. Besides, the doctor will never let you leave the hospital until you are healed."

"You can sneaked me out."

Sarah's heart skipped a beat. Would nothing stop this kid's determination?

"Um, how would I do that?"

"You can hide me in your dress and walk that way." He nodded toward the front door.

"I don't think there is that much room under my dress." She chuckled. "I don't think that plan would work."

"Then I will ask Doctor Stimson if I can go home now."

She giggled again. "You are a rascally little one, aren't you?" She brushed back his hair.

"I'm leaving whether you help me or not."

Sarah sat up straight. Carson's tone was so willful and he sounded like a boy twice his age. She felt cornered and a little scared that Carson would get out. Then what? He didn't know where James was. How would he get there? He would certainly meet his end trying to find James.

"Honey, I think that's enough for now. Why don't you get some rest and we'll talk again in the morning." She started to kiss his cheek before she left.

Carson turned away from her. "I'll do it."

Sarah sighed. She heard James in Carson's voice. That strong-willed determination of a young man who wants to leave a mark on the world. A young man who has no idea how much danger exists out there. A young man who has only thought things out so far. James had always been quite a handful. Now she had to deal with Carson? Sarah thought she had finally graduated from caring for impetuous little boys.

"Carson, your condition is very serious. You are bandaged up. You can only use one arm. And what about all the blood you have lost? You just aren't strong enough to go on an adventure right now." She rubbed his left arm.

Carson stared at her with an angry expression. It was more than a pout. It had violence behind it. Sarah quivered with a tinge of fear. She wondered if the boy had become possessed.

"I am going."

"No, you're not."

"Yes, I am."

"No, you're not."

"YES I AM!" He screamed.

Sarah looked around as the other patients and visitors stared at them. Her cheeks reddened and she lowered her voice to Carson.

"What do you want from me?"

"I want you to take me to James."

"I can't."

"Then I will go by myself."

Sarah squeezed Carson's arm tight. She didn't even realize she was doing it until he squirmed away shouting, "Ouch." She rubbed the arm where her grip had been.

"Fine."

Carson's expression brightened.

"Fine. You boys are going to be the death of me."

Carson smiled.

Sarah tried to guilt him. It had worked so many times with James.

"I will get you to James, if I don't get caught and end up in jail for the rest of my days."

Carson kept smiling.

"Hopefully, I won't fall down and break my leg or get bitten by a rattlesnake."

He was still smiling.

"Of course, I don't know how I will bring you back to town once the gunslinger kills me."

Carson's expression was unchanged.

She couldn't believe it. Her powers were useless on the special child. Sarah sighed and looked out the window. Now she was in a corner. Good going, Sarah. She pinched her leg to teach herself a lesson.

"Very well. I will go home and pack some things. And see if I can find us a horse. Then I will be back to get you."

Carson's eyes sparkled with delight.

"Now don't you go and say anything about this to the doctor or the nurses. Not anyone. If they know what we're fixin' to do, they will stop us before we start." Part of her hoped putting the idea in his head would be enough for him to slip up. Then they could avoid this dangerous undertaking.

Sarah bent to kiss his cheek. She brushed his hair back and told him she would be back in a bit. As she left the hospital, her mind flashed all kinds of horrific scenarios. Getting lost in the dark. Falling off the horse. Finding a tribe of wild Indians. Getting robbed, or worse, by a gang of hooligans. There was no end to the possibilities. And none of them were good.

She brushed a bead of sweat from her brow as she tried to ignore more nightmarish thoughts.

CHAPTER 38

James couldn't shake the ghostly images of the gunslinger's family. Each time he sifted through a new section of ash and rubble, he imagined the skeletons. He feared that a charred, bony hand would reach out and grasp his arm. A shudder wriggled down his legs as he kicked over what must have been some pots and pans.

He stretched his back, which was beginning to ache. A jostling horseback ride followed by lots of bending and lifting had knotted up his muscles. James looked over his shoulder. Sheriff Morgan was clearing away debris on his hands and knees.

James faced the setting sun and admired the beautiful landscape. The fields met the sky at the horizon, a yellowed crisp against an orange canvas. He thought about how strange it was. The setting was so beautiful. Yet, the work they needed to finish was dark. And morbid. He lifted his hat and patted down his face with the back of his sleeve.

"You gonna daydream all day or are you gonna dig in?"

James rolled his eyes at the Sheriff before bending back to work. He rolled another pot over and then continued clearing away dust. The thought of wasting time crossed his mind. They knew they were searching for some sort of connection. But neither of them knew what it could be.

A few minutes later, James found a book. It had a cloth cover and was covered with years of dirt. He brushed the soil from the jacket and tried to make out the print. The title was too worn to figure out what it said. James leafed through the book, which seemed to contain hand drawn pictures on each page. Some of the drawings focused on detailed backgrounds. An expanse of field. A morning sunrise over the tree line. Others captured objects that tried to tell a story. Like the hand ax sticking out of a stump. Or the chicken pecking at seeds in the center of her little chicks.

James thought the drawings were rich and stunning. He couldn't recall a time when he had witnessed such perfect art work. He secretly wished he could draw pictures. He thought he would show himself slaying giants and saving cattle from drowning in a deep stream. Real cowboy hero pictures.

As he flipped through the collection, a yellowed square of paper fell out. It drifted to the sand at his feet. James stared at it. He almost didn't believe what he saw. He squatted down and picked up an old photograph. It was very dirty and he rubbed his thumb over it to clean it up a bit.

James' eyes absorbed each face. He assumed the picture was Doddy with his wife and daughter. The man standing in front of the homestead looked like the gunslinger. Well, James thought, if the gunslinger still had flesh on his face. The cheekbones were well pronounced, accentuated further by the thick, black sideburns. The pencil thin mustache rested above the unsmiling mouth. James noticed the same black pants with the vest. The man's hat was rounded and flat, just like the gunslinger's. There was no doubt, in James' mind, that this was him.

The woman wore a long, patterned dress which covered her feet. Her hands were clasped together in front of her waist. She, too, wore no smile. Her hair appeared to be lighter in color than Doddy's. She had it braided down each shoulder like an Indian princess. Although, James could tell by her complexion she was not Indian. Her eyes seemed set far apart over a narrow nose. It made her look a bit unattractive.

James' eyes followed over to the young girl. Thin arms hung down at her sides. Her skin appeared overly white, like a spoonful of butter cream. The little girl's hair was long and straight. Like her mother, she had lighter colored hair. The striking difference was in the eyes. Unlike her parents, Sally's eyes sparkled with wonderment. Her head was tilted back slightly and her smile encompassed her face. It looked like she was laughing when the photograph was taken.

After studying the picture, James couldn't help feeling sorry for the gunslinger. As bad as he was in death, Doddy was an ordinary man. Just a hardworking farmer who did his best for his small family. He and Martha looked tired and serious in stark contrast to the precociousness of little Sally. James swallowed a lump in his throat as he wished he had had a normal upbringing like Sally. James had never met his father. And he and his mother had always lived in small quarters above saloons. They never had a place in the wild with land to farm and raise animals. He felt jealous that he never knew that side of life.

"Whatcha got there, kid?" Sheriff Morgan walked up to James.

James was still a little choked up so he just waved the photograph in front of the Sheriff. He accepted the picture from James, as he looked it over with a nod.

"That's them, alright. Sally. Martha. Doddy." The Sheriff brushed the photo against his chest to clear the rest of the dust. "It's a shame they had to die like that." He handed the picture back to James, and then lit a cigarette. "Think that'll help?"

James handed Sheriff Morgan the tattered book. "I don't know what to think. I guess I hope it'll mean something."

"Yeah, well I don't know how much you can reason with a spirit. But it's worth a shot. Nothing else has worked yet."

James took the book back from the Sheriff when he had finished flipping through the pages. He tucked the photograph inside the book. James wasn't sure how any of this wreckage was going to help. He started to second guess his decision to chase the gunslinger. It felt like the choices he made got incrementally worse.

"Night will be falling soon. Best get a fire started for us. You finish sifting through this junk while I get us situated."

Sheriff Morgan left James alone with his thoughts. He brushed his boot back and forth over the garbage. Then he clutched the book and stared at it some more.

CHAPTER 39

Eleanor entered Miller's General Store in a panic. It was late and she knew that Mr. Miller would be closing up shortly. She needed to pick up some ingredients for the cake she was making. Tomorrow would be a special day for the children in class because several of them would be moving on to a higher level of arithmetic. Eleanor chose to make a big deal of accomplishments so the children stayed excited about learning.

She greeted Mr. Miller as she hurried between the rows of shelves.

"Take your time, Miss Lark. I'm not in any hurry to close."

"Oh, thank you, Mr. Miller."

"Please. Call me, Ed. I've told you countless times to just call me Ed." Mr. Miller smiled at her as he approached. "Maybe I can help you find what you are looking for?"

"Oh, yes. That would be wonderful." She tried to catch her breath as she shared her list with Ed. He looked over the ingredients and started to collect the items from his shelves. Eleanor relaxed a bit and followed him around the store.

"Looks like someone is baking a cake. Special occasion?"

"Yes, the school children are celebrating an achievement tomorrow.

So I thought I would bring something sweet to eat." She smiled and clasped her hands together.

"If I had a teacher as thoughtful as you when I was a boy, I might have lasted more than a few months."

"Don't be silly. A successful businessman like you must have gone through more education than a few months."

"I actually didn't."

Eleanor dropped her jaw in shock. Mr. Miller rounded an aisle and kept searching for her items while he continued.

"I dropped out because I was "too good" for school. So my old man punished me for dropping out. He put me to work on his farm and he gave me the worst jobs imaginable. Cleaning out the chicken coops. Digging water wells. Working the mules with the cultivator. Hard labor for a little boy."

"Oh my. That's terrible."

"Not completely. It taught me the value of hard work. And it gave me a reason to search for something better. I decided at a young age that I wanted to be on my own. Not taking orders from some grumpy old guy."

Eleanor laughed and Ed grinned at her. He placed the last item in the box and carried it to the counter. As he tallied up the items, Eleanor glanced out the window at the quieting street activity.

"I guess everyone is heading home for the day."

"Yeah. Well, those of us fortunate enough to be heading home."

Eleanor looked at Ed with an expression of confusion. He noticed as he finished scrawling on the ledger. "You know what I mean. Everyone except Sheriff Morgan and James."

She continued to screw up her face as she struggled to understand what Ed was talking about.

"I'm sorry. I thought you knew they were going to chase down the haunted gunslinger."

"Oh, yes. Well, I mean, I knew they were going to do it. I just didn't realize it would be so soon."

"Yep. They left earlier today. Came in here for some supplies and took off for the old Doddy place."

"I see." Eleanor placed her hand against her cheek in dismay. She couldn't believe James had left without saying goodbye. What if something awful happened to him? And she never got a chance to see him one last time? She worried that the last time they saw each other it was under stressful circumstances. The little fight they had would be the last memory she would have of James.

"Is something wrong, Miss Lark?"

Eleanor was lost in thought but snapped back to the present. "Um, no. I just thought of something that I didn't do."

"Well, there's always tomorrow, right?"

She nodded without confidence. There was always tomorrow for some things. But not for telling someone that you care about them. Not for letting them know that you…love them? Eleanor was surprised at the conclusion her train of thought had arrived at. Did she love James? She hardly knew him. Yes, she thought he was handsome. And she enjoyed being around him. He was so nice and courteous. But love? Her cheeks reddened.

"Miss Lark?"

"What?"

"Are you okay?"

"Yes, why do you ask?" Her breath came out in gasps.

"You just looked like you drifted off somewhere."

"Oh." She tried to recover. "I just realized something else. Um, something else I forgot to do. I'm sorry, Mr. Miller." She noticed him tilting his head at her in correction. "Sorry. Ed."

Mr. Miller smiled at her and wished her a good evening. He handed her the small box of sundries and she left the store. Ed locked the door behind her and waved through the window. She smiled back and stepped into the street with her goods.

Eleanor started to cry.

She couldn't believe she had fallen in love with James. Since she was a little girl, she had always dreamed of marrying a man of position. A ranked officer in the army or a wealthy landowner. Not a stock boy. And he was younger than she. What would people say about the spinster school teacher who found love in a younger man? She was only older by a handful of years but it would still be considered scandalous. Besides, James didn't feel the same way towards her. She thought he seemed to like her, too. But the way things left off when Sarah threw her out of the room didn't support that notion. It was too abrupt and James hadn't run after her. Nor had he bothered to check in with her before he went on a dangerous trip.

Her heart sank. The tears flowed quicker as she hurried her pace to get home. She hoped nobody would find her in such a state. It was bad enough that she was crushed. Then to have to explain herself or worse, lie to cover up her true emotions would be terrible.

She cried harder as her pace quickened. The last time she had seen James he wore a scowl and he was upset. Eleanor didn't want to go on living if James died tonight without her telling him how she felt. Her lost love trickled down her cheeks.

CHAPTER 40

Sheriff Morgan belched and waved a hand past his own face. James smiled at the funny gesture. It made him think of Carson. Sometimes, when they ate together, they would burp out loud and then blow it into each other's faces. The goal was to completely sicken the other with sound and smell. Carson usually doubled over with deep belly laughs when James did it. He missed Carson badly.

They ate in silence, as the flames danced between them. James tried to squeeze Carson out of his mind. But it was no use. He kept seeing Carson bumping into him from behind or slapping down a winning hand of cards. And flying backwards after being shot. James' stomach twisted with the memory.

"You're awfully quiet." The Sheriff extended another chunk of bread to James.

James shrugged and took the bread. He broke off a piece and chewed it, as he studied the flames. "You ever regret something so bad it makes your stomach hurt?"

The Sheriff stopped chewing while he stared at James. "Are you serious?"

James reddened. He felt foolish for opening up to this tough man about his feelings.

"Only on days that end in 'Y'."

James furrowed his brow and then figured out the joke. He laughed and Sheriff Morgan joined in. Suddenly, James felt more at ease.

"Why do you think I'm out here with you? It ain't yer conversational skills."

"Thank you."

The Sheriff laughed again.

"I just...I just want to take care of Carson. Except I make things more difficult for him."

"How so?"

"Well, he wants to go everywhere I go and do everything I do. But the things I do ain't safe for a boy like him."

"What do you mean, a boy like him?"

"You know..." James let the response drift without finishing it.

"The pastor says that God only gives us what we can handle. Do you believe that, James?"

"I guess so. I haven't been to services in a while."

"Well, if you believe God only gives us as much as we can handle, then don't you think Carson is doing okay?"

James looked up at Sheriff Morgan. "I never thought of it like that."

"Time to think of it like that then, son. Carson took two slugs and he is on the mend. I think that means God feels that boy can handle a lot more than you give him credit for."

James watched the flames. He realized Sheriff Morgan was right. All this time he worried about protecting Carson from the world around him. But Carson was strong enough to take care of himself. Well, in most cases. He was slower than many others but it never SLOWED him down from wanting the same life as James. He couldn't believe he hadn't seen it until now. James smiled.

"So what do you regret? Every day, by the sounds of it?" James wanted to shift the conversation away from himself.

Sheriff Morgan tossed the last morsel of bread into the fire and wiped his hands down his pants. He looked at the sky while he finished chewing what was left in his mouth. "This."

James screwed up his face. "Sitting under the stars?"

"No. This. This mission. What happened to Doddy and his kin."

"It wasn't your fault though."

"Wasn't it? I killed Doddy with my own hands. And now look what he's done to our town and all the good people." Sheriff Morgan lowered his head.

"But the men burned his home and killed his family. They did all this." James opened his arms to indicate the rubble around them.

"Yeah, well I could have stopped things sooner. But I didn't."

Both men watched the flames flicker and pop. Silence filled the air when the critters paused in their cacophony.

"I should have done something sooner. I knew it was heading down the wrong path. But I kept my mouth shut. I played along by not standing up for what I believed in. I let Doddy down. And I let myself down."

James wanted to say something else to convince Sheriff Morgan it wasn't his fault. But the Sheriff didn't give him a chance.

"That little girl was a lot like your brother, Carson. She was very…special." The words followed some sparks that fizzled to the night sky. "She was an angel in a dress. The sweetest creature you could ever meet. People knew she was not like the rest of us. That's one of the reasons Doddy brought her out here."

James blinked as he listened to this fascinating new information.

"Sally drew those pictures in that book, you know. She could barely speak but she had the Lord's voice in her fingertips."

James was stunned that the little six-year old had created the amazing art. He figured it was Martha or Doddy who had done it.

"Real special kid. And to see her burnt up like a slab of meat…not a day goes by where I don't see her laying there in the pile…it wasn't right for me to keep quiet for my job…that little, innocent child died because of me."

James heard the crack in the Sheriff's voice. He struggled to confess his involvement to James. He pitied the Sheriff as much as he did the gunslinger and his family. James thought to himself that he had always believed evil came from evil people. After Crouching Bear and the gunslinger, James was finding it more difficult to define evil. And where it came from.

"Reckon I'll answer for my sins sooner or later."

"I think you'll handle what you've been given." James tried to make the Sheriff feel better.

Sheriff Morgan looked at James. He saw the tears in his eyes. The Sheriff nodded and threw some more wood on the fire. "That's what I'm afraid of."

They spent the next few hours in silence. The canopy of stars brought the heavens within reach and James thought about their purpose. He wondered if he would get a chance to see Carson again. If he did, he promised himself he would include Carson as an equal instead of protecting him for being slow. He could just imagine Carson's face when he told him how things would be different.

CHAPTER 41

The road to the farm was very difficult for Sarah and Carson. The darkness encroached upon their trail, making the landmarks hard to recognize. They plodded on under the stars at a slow pace. Two riders on one horse was uncomfortable, at best. Adding Carson's bandaged upper body only contributed to the discomfort.

After Sarah left Carson's bedside, she had quietly found a regular customer at the brothel who was willing to lend her a horse. She was able to get Ginger to cover for her, as Madam, for the evening while she "took care of an important family matter." The girls knew what had happened to Carson. Hell, everyone in town knew what had happened so it was easy enough to find an excuse to get out of working.

Sarah packed a small sack of garments and some jerky and water. Then she waited for night to fall so she could sneak Carson out the back door of the hospital. Sarah was relieved that it had been easier than she had thought it would be. Since most of the patients slept at night, the nursing staff decreased during the evening hours. Apparently, the night nurse on duty spent most of her shift occupying the desk in the front of the building while the patients slept. So Sarah watched through the windows until her opportunity arose. She quietly opened the back door and carried Carson out to the awaiting horse.

She couldn't believe how heavy Carson had been. The boy looked so frail and slight, even when he was fully healthy. But he felt like a huge sack of flour. Sarah managed to hoist Carson up on the horse without too many complaints, even when his injured arm brushed the pommel. Then she hopped on behind him and kept Carson inside her arms for extra protection. It was custom for a lady to ride side-saddle with both legs on the same side, but Sarah cussed under her breath that she wasn't a lady like that "in times like these." She straddled the horse and rode with the front of her dress bunched up against her belly.

The trail was mostly flat. Once in awhile large rocks littered the path, forcing them to go slowly to avoid being thrown. Sarah made sure to stop every ten or fifteen minutes to check on Carson and readjust their seating arrangement. She utilized the breaks to reconfirm their bearings as well. She hadn't traveled like this at night in years. She had forgotten how treacherous and scary it was. The fear of going off in the wrong direction. The howls of coyotes and other wild beasts startling her. Plus a general sense of unease, as if dangerous men were out there, somewhere, watching them and waiting to ambush them. Sarah knew these fears were mostly unfounded. She chalked it up to town living and becoming accustomed to lots of people and civilized noises.

"I have to pee."

Sarah pulled the reins back and the horse stopped. She slid down and helped Carson dismount. Once again his arm brushed the pommel and he whined about the pain. Sarah apologized and helped him take a few steps off the trail to relieve himself. As Carson's pee pattered upon the rocks and sand, Sarah realized she could use a break too. She rounded the other side of the horse, lifted her dress up and squatted down over the trail. A steady stream of urine flowed and she sighed with relief. Before she could finish, she heard Carson making his way slowly back in her direction.

"Hold on, Carson. I'll be right there." She finished up and met Carson who stood groggily in the dark. "You want something to eat before we get going again?"

"Uh-uh." Carson yawned out loud and Sarah began lifting him back onto the horse. She got him situated and then climbed up. As soon as she sat against him, Sarah felt Carson lean back into her breasts. His head angled to the side like he was readying for sleep. She smiled at the wonderful feeling of a young child nuzzling up to her. She thought about how many years had gone by since James had done this with her. She missed it greatly. Sarah chose to enjoy the affectionate comfort of Carson while she had it. She kissed his greasy hair and clucked to get the horse moving again.

Sarah began to feel like this was the right thing to do. She hated herself for allowing Carson to get to her. She felt an overpowering desire to protect Carson as if he were her own child. For all intents, he was her child now. But she had given in to his strong demands and taken him away from the hospital. Somewhere deep inside, she was trying to reconcile Carson's and James' relationship with each other. And that desire won out.

Her thoughts trickled back to James and how much he had grown up. She knew the boy was gone, replaced by a man. A man who craved adventure and life in the wild. There was nothing she could do to protect him anymore or deter him from getting himself into trouble. All she could do was advise him. And pray for him. Maybe there would be some consolation in taking care of Carson. He provided her with another focus to feed her motherly instincts.

"Momma."

Carson mumbled as he drifted to sleep. Sarah saddened as he called for her old friend, Minnie. She thought about Carson's mother for the first time in a while, since she had died. Tears filled her eyes as she remembered all the times they had laughed together, talked about their boys and looked out for each other. Minnie had been like family to Sarah. Which made taking care of Carson that much more important to her.

"You're my momma now."

Sarah was stunned. She couldn't believe what Carson had just said. He was actually cooing to her, not calling for his birth mother. Sarah's eyes overflowed with tears and she tried to sniffle quietly so Carson wouldn't know she was crying. She kissed his head again and squeezed him into her breasts, while she pulled back the reins.

She was doing the right thing after all. She was bringing her boys together. Where they belonged. With each other.

"My little boy." Sarah whispered into Carson's hair and rode on, while he slept in her arms.

CHAPTER 42

"Time to start." Sheriff Morgan punched James in the shoulder. It was a friendly punch, like two buddies might give each other as they hung out, swapping stories and jokes. Only Sheriff Morgan's strength delivered pain, which radiated from James' shoulder down to his fingertips.

He yawned with his mouth wide open. Wide enough to swallow the moon. His hand instinctively touched the handle of the six-shooter tucked into the back of his belt loop. The feel of the gun had become a source of comfort for James. Whenever he felt scared or apprehensive, he would reach around to touch his gun. And then everything would feel better.

James looked at the fire and wondered if there was a way he could get out of this. The butterflies in his stomach floated in chaotic orbits, making the bile grow. He swallowed a huge lump in his throat. The time for fighting had arrived.

Sheriff Morgan retrieved his rifle from the saddle pouch. He cocked the lever to chamber a round. He put the rifle on the ground and took out his sidearm. He opened the cylinder and checked all the rounds, closed it up and spun the cylinder around before re-holstering the gun.

James watched him prepare his firearms. He glanced down at the family portrait that he had pulled from the tattered book. The serious expressions haunted him. And Sally's laugh still frozen in time, sent shivers down his spine.

"I'm ready."

James nodded over his shoulder at Sheriff Morgan. He placed the faded photograph back in the book and clutched it as if he were afraid to let it drop from his grasp. James took several deep breaths and then began to coax the spirit to reveal itself. A last moment thought ran through his mind that they had assumed they would be able to draw out the gunslinger from anywhere. But what if it could only be done back in town? Near the clock tower? Too late now, he thought.

"Come on out, gunslinger."

Nothing but silence answered James.

"You said you knew how to find me. Remember that? Well, here I am."

James realized all the sounds of nature around them had disappeared. No more crickets, coyotes. Silence. It was eerie. Even the slight breeze had evaporated. The air was still. Just an occasional crackle from the fire.

He looked over his shoulder at the Sheriff, who was stoic, with his rifle in his hands. The Sheriff nodded ever so slightly at James.

"You wanted respect. So I'm here to show you that I respect you. And what happened to your family." He looked around, sensing a change in the atmosphere. A low, vibration trembled below the surface of the earth. It worked its way through his boots. He swallowed again.

"Revenge then? Is that what you really seek?"

A breeze kicked up swirls of dust. It was stronger than the gentle wind of earlier. This air brought portents of evil.

"I'm here to deliver your revenge. And put your soul at ease." James looked over his shoulder again. Sheriff Morgan's jaw hung wide. James grinned and nodded, trying to reassure the Sheriff he wasn't giving him up to the gunslinger. But James did plan on using the Sheriff as his wild card.

The gunslinger buzzed into view, amid the static crackles and pops that filled the air. Just as he always looked, the gunslinger stood opposite James, on the other side of the fire.

James stared into the black pits that stood where the gunslinger's eyes should be. Another chill worked its way through him. He squeezed the dirty book in his hand.

"What took you so long?"

The gunslinger grinned, a sinewy, skeletal grin. The thin strip of black mustache stretched above the lip-less mouth.

"This needs to end. Tonight."

The gunslinger didn't respond. He just stood with his hands at his sides. The bony jaw wriggled left to right as he gritted his rotted teeth.

James wanted to get this over with. The impatient side of him wanted to draw down on the gunslinger and try to end the conflict. Regardless of him surviving the battle or not. But the frightened side of him thought more about running until he reached a place where no ghosts existed. The outcome would fall somewhere in between, James figured.

"Shame what happened to your family."

The gunslinger stood motionless.

"Nobody deserves to die like that. Least of all a wife and a little girl."

A rumbling groan emanated from the gunslinger.

"You only did what any good family man would have done."

The gunslinger tossed his duster back so both pistols were within reach.

James felt the cold sweat line his upper lip. His heart palpitated. It became increasingly more difficult for James to breathe. His eyes focused on the gunslinger's hands. He knew there would be little time to react if he went for the six-shooters.

"Let's handle this like men. Like smart men. Okay?"

The gunslinger laughed, sending goosebumps across James' flesh. The sound was loud and pierced right through the core of his brain. James did all he could to avoid dropping to his knees while clutching his ears. He heard Sheriff Morgan shift behind him.

When the laugh finally ceased, James held up his hands in mock surrender. He wanted to show the gunslinger he wasn't a threat. Not yet, at least. He hoped he could stay alive long enough to figure out how to take advantage of a moment of weakness.

The gunslinger tilted his head to the side, as if he were trying to figure out what James was doing. James realized the gunslinger was staring at his hand. The one holding the tattered book. Maybe the gunslinger recognized the jacket, even though it was marred with years of dust and ash.

One bony finger stretched out in his direction. It stopped when it pointed directly at the book in James' upturned hand. He knew the gunslinger saw it. There was no putting the juice back in the jar now. James wondered if the timing was right to share his find with the gunslinger.

His decision was made for him. The gunslinger maintained his position, with finger outstretched, pointing at the book. James knew he had arrived at the point of no return.

CHAPTER 43

"Psst!"

James heard Sheriff Morgan try to get his attention. But he couldn't take his eyes off the gunslinger. James' legs were rooted to the ground. His body stiffened, alert to any imperceptible movements that might indicate he was about to be shot at. James felt like a sitting duck.

"Psst!"

"Not now, dangit." James bristled at letting the cuss word out.

The gunslinger took a few steps toward James, finger still pointing at the book.

"Take it easy, now."

"What is that in your hand?" The gravelly voice was almost a whisper.

"This is a book."

"I'm not blind, James. What kind of book?"

"Um, it is a journal or something. With drawings in it."

The gunslinger lowered his finger. James felt relief that it wasn't pointing at the book. Then he tensed when he realized both hands were closer to those guns now.

"Where did you find it?"

"Here. In the remains of your homestead."

"What makes you think this was my homestead?" The ghost moved closer.

"Well, you're Doddy aren't you? Uh, weren't you? I mean."

The gunslinger stared at James. The black eye sockets gave him another shiver. James wondered if the gunslinger was truly Doddy. He almost doubted it for a second. Especially after the gunslinger's question. But it had to be him. The apparition looked exactly like the man in the old photograph.

"Let me see that book."

"Why? If you aren't Doddy, then what do you care what this book contains?"

The gunslinger growled. "Curiosity, perhaps."

James laughed. He tried to stop it from coming out but it was so startlingly absurd to him that a ghost could be curious about anything, let alone a book. He quickly cut his laugh off when he saw the expression change on the gunslinger's face.

"You laughing at me, boy?"

"No. No, no. I'm just…something tickled me is all." James swallowed a lump that could choke a horse. "But it is you, isn't it? Francis Dodson?"

The gunslinger's eyebrows furrowed. "Francis Dodson is dead." The statement carried finality in its tone.

"The living Francis Dodson is dead. Sure. But the spirit still lives. Doesn't it?"

"What are you driving at, James?" When the gunslinger said his name, it lingered for several seconds in a breathy, horrific sound.

"You're Doddy. Or used to be." James finally lowered his arms. He felt the exhaustion in his shoulders. He opened the book and removed the old photograph. "You're right here. In this photograph. Plain and simple."

James turned the photo toward the gunslinger and held it out so the flames would expose the image. The gunslinger leaned forward, black eyes squinting to get a better look.

"Give me that."

"No. If you aren't Doddy, you have no use for this picture."

"Give it to me now!" The voice thundered. James felt his chest vibrate from the loud roar. He suddenly had an urge to relieve himself, but he got it under control. The gunslinger got a little closer.

"I don't fault you for wanting to avenge your family. Martha. Sally. She was beautiful."

"What do you know about family, boy? You ever been in love? You ever hold a tiny creature that came from a small part of you? You know nothin'." The gunslinger spat the words out with vitriol.

"Sally was so talented. The drawings...they are so life-like. I can't believe a little girl could create something so beautiful."

"Don't...talk...about Sally."

"She was special to you, wasn't she?"

The gunslinger groaned and inched closer. "Give me that book."

James took a step back and then thought he better stand his ground. He didn't want the gunslinger to know he was scared. So James recovered and took a step forward again.

He flipped through the tattered book so the gunslinger might get glimpses of the incredible artwork. The pages fluttered, puffing small clumps of dirt and dust as they turned.

The gunslinger leaned forward again to spy the lost pages. He groaned and then whimpered. At least, James thought he heard a whimper. It was soft but audible. James watched the gunslinger's face and he saw the eyebrows upturned like a child who cried over a skinned knee.

"Sally." The word croaked from the trembling mouth of the gunslinger.

"She was perfect. Pretty. Talented. Special. Wasn't she?"

The gunslinger shook with what appeared to be deep sorrow. His hands outstretched slowly to beg for the book. His head lowered so the brim of the flat hat covered his face. James definitely picked up on sobs now.

"But she was different. And that's why you moved her out here. Away from all the insults and name-calling."

"She wasn't...different." The gunslinger sobbed and choked. "She was BETTER than everyone else." The words screamed through James' soul. His chest vibrated again.

"Yes. Better than everyone. And you only did what you had to do to protect her and care for her. Until they took her from you."

The gunslinger stood up straight. His face toughened and he growled. Low at first and then growing in volume.

"You tried to avenge her but it didn't work out. And now you have to move on. Be with her now."

"NO! Noooooooooooooooooooooooo!" The booming sound knocked James off his feet. As he rolled over, he saw Sheriff Morgan also in the dirt. Both men scrambled back to their feet as quickly as they could, but cautiously enough to keep the gunslinger from drawing upon them.

"Sally wants you to be near her. All you have to do is go. Leave this old town and go to your family."

"I can't."

"Why not?"

The gunslinger took another step closer. His hands rested upon the gun handles now. "Because I made a promise to hunt down everyone. Everyone that played a hand in my family's deaths."

"Promises can be broken. Especially old promises." James thought to himself he was living proof of that. He had promised Carson they would do things together and look how many times he had broken all those promises.

"Not this promise."

James watched the gunslinger's hands carefully. He sensed the gunslinger was teetering on the brink of self-control. He didn't know how much time they had left to figure out this haunting.

"I made a deal with the devil."

CHAPTER 44

The faint glow of a camp fire flickered to the northeast. At least, Sarah thought it looked like a possibility. She hoped that was the destination because she was weary and the trip seemed to take longer than she had expected. She had known it would take them longer to arrive than it normally would because they were traveling at night and going slow on purpose to avoid mishaps with Carson but it seemed unusually long.

Carson was still sleeping. Sarah figured the repetitive motion of the horse had lulled the boy to sleep. Plus, he was still weak from blood loss and recovering from two gun wounds. She shook her head as she thought of Carson's resiliency. Ah, to be young and energetic, she thought. Sarah wasn't particularly old but she didn't have the reserves she had possessed years ago.

She kicked her feet to spur the horse to pick up the pace. She worried that the horse would make too much noise though. She didn't want to alert the folks if they weren't James and Sheriff Morgan. And, if it was them, she still wanted to sneak up just in case the scene was chaotic.

As they neared the site, Sarah smelled the wood burning first. Then she identified the flickering light of a camp fire. She hoped this was it.

The location was roughly where they were headed but everything was so difficult to see in the darkness. Sarah slowed the horse again to deafen any potential noise.

Sarah thought there were some people standing around but she couldn't be sure. Might just be shadows playing tricks on her eyes. They were about fifty yards away now. Sarah stopped the horse and slid off, careful to lean Carson forward gently. His head rested on the horse's neck. She kept her hand on Carson's back for a few minutes in order to maintain the sensation of her warmth and touch. Just in case he stirred from her movement, she figured he might drift off again knowing that her body was still within reach.

Sarah let go of Carson and draped a wool blanket over his small frame. She quietly tied the horse's reins to a scrub bush that was sparse. She hoped it was alive enough to anchor the horse if it got spooked.

She brushed her hair back behind her ears to keep her vision clear. As she crouched over, Sarah began to wind her way through thickets and sporadic groves. She was careful to step slowly so she minimized any sound. Her eyes never strayed from the flickering light. A pit formed in her stomach as dread began to work its way through her system. Sarah couldn't explain why the feelings arose. She just felt that something was different in this vicinity. Something felt…off.

Her legs began to tremble. The sensation seemed to come up through the earth though. It didn't originate in her body, which only heightened her sense of dread.

Sarah arrived close enough to make out the shadows. They weren't shadows at all. It was James with the Sheriff a few feet behind him. And on the other side of the fire stood the gunslinger. A breath caught in her throat, as she gasped. It had worked. James had been able to summon the spirit to the farm. Even though she understood their plan, she was still surprised that it had worked. She had some doubts since the apparition only appeared annually in the town's main thoroughfare.

She strained to make out the conversation but she was too far away. She estimated she was still a good twenty yards or so from the fire. Another tremble in the earth wiggled its way up her legs. Sarah wondered what caused the disturbance, figuring it must have something to do with the gunslinger and the charged atmosphere. It was a sensation she had never felt before.

The gunslinger made a sound that reminded Sarah of a roar. The noise shook the area and trees and plants swayed to the shock waves. A chill shot down Sarah's spine and reversed course to her brain. She felt a little disoriented. Sarah thought of Carson. He was still behind with the horse. Her motherly instincts kicked in. Sarah wanted to get back to Carson to keep him from waking. She knew if he awoke, he would demand to be by James' side. Now wasn't the time. With the gunslinger here.

Sarah spun on her heels and made her way through the dense foliage. Another earthly tremble shivered across the plain. The wail of a saddened voice echoed across the expanse. She had no idea what the words were. But she knew whatever was taking place behind, or was about to take place, was no place for Carson.

She hoped she could keep Carson out of range of the sights and sounds of the farm for as long as possible. Part of her was glad they had arrived after the gunslinger. Otherwise, poor Carson would be in the middle of it all with James right now. And the thought of both boys in harm's way made her sick to her stomach. No mother should have to bury a child. But two children? She shuttered at the prospect of a deadly evening. Sarah started whispering prayers as she made her way back to the horse.

As Sarah reached the shrub, she saw the horse was still tethered to it. But nobody sat on the horse. Sarah's eyes grew wide as she panicked and searched for Carson. She ran to the horse and looked underneath. She circled the animal and then the shrub. Nothing. Where could he be? How could Carson have disappeared? He was fast asleep, right here, she screamed to herself. Sarah turned in circles, looking for anything that might provide cover for a sleeping or hiding child. She began calling his name. Softly at first, almost a whisper. But each time her voice got louder as more fear settled in. Where could he be?

No sooner did she have the thought, than Sarah realized. Carson went to James. She knew deep in her gut that the rascally boy had woken up and noticed the fire, and had probably made his way back there. She couldn't believe she was so foolish to leave him all alone. In the darkness. An injured little boy. A determined, injured little boy.

Sarah glowered in the direction of the camp fire. She knew where Carson was. And she had to go get him.

CHAPTER 45

The gunslinger straightened. James watched as the saddened, slumped figure transformed into an imposing threat. He had confessed to his deal with the devil in order to avenge his family's deaths. So the spirit of Doddy was trapped in a state of unrest. Never joining the souls of his family in the afterlife. James felt sorry for him. But his sympathy wouldn't get in the way of saving the townspeople from the demon.

James tried one more time to bargain for peace. "Look, I'll give you Sally's book and the old photograph if you promise to go away and never come back to town."

"How about you give me the book and the photograph and I fill your rotten gut with slugs?"

"That doesn't sound like a fair trade at all."

"And when you take your last breath, I will consume your soul while your dying eyes watch. Then I will go back and rid the rest of the town of its guilty lives."

"Sounds like you want a fight." James tried to remain brave, but swallowed a lump just the same.

"Won't be much of a fight."

The gunslinger sprung for his six-shooters. In a flash, he had pulled the guns from their leather sheaths and raised the barrels at James. It happened so fast but James managed to drop to the dirt before any bullets hit him. Two shots fired. One from each barrel.

When James hit the ground he heard a thump behind him. He turned and watched Sheriff Morgan flop down in a spray of blood. The Sheriff got hit with at least one of the shots meant for his own body. Before getting up, James realized he had lost the tattered book with the photograph in it. He must have dropped it when he fell down. There was no time to look for it now.

James spun on one knee and drew the pistol from the back of his belt. He swung it around and fired right away. The bullet caught the gunslinger off guard and smacked dead center into his chest. The only problem was the bullet passed through without doing any damage. James recalled the Sheriff's shot passing through the gunslinger's belly. If the torso was not vulnerable, then maybe the head would be.

The gunslinger fired two more shots toward James. He rolled over and hid behind a collapsed section of porch. The wood might not stop the gunslinger's bullets completely, but James hoped it would at least slow them down. The shots danced through the dirt, sending puffs of dust into the night air.

James heard Sheriff Morgan struggle behind him. He watched the Sheriff rise to his knees with his rifle aimed at the gunslinger. The Sheriff's teeth were red, his mouth full of blood from an internal injury. James noticed the bloody stain on the front of the Sheriff's vest. A gut shot. The Sheriff yelled something unintelligible and fired a round. He cranked the lever to chamber another one and fired again.

The gunslinger changed his position to level his barrels at the Sheriff. He easily dodged the volley coming his way and he let loose two more shots at the lawman. James screamed "No," as he watched the two bullets hit the mark. One slapped into Sheriff Morgan's stomach with a wet sound. The other thudded into his chest, spewing blood up to the stars in a fine mist. Sheriff Axl Morgan's eyes met James' in a moment that seemed to last an eternity. James thought the Sheriff's expression showed relief, like his soul would finally be unburdened by the sins of the past. The wrinkles beside his eyes came together in a smirk. A faint smile painted the Sheriff's bloody lips as he slumped backwards into the soil.

"NOOOOOOOOOOO!" James screamed again and jumped to his feet. He fired three shots at the gunslinger, as he charged at the evil spirit. One shot missed wide. Another hit the gunslinger's shoulder, passing through without damage. The third bullet hit the gunslinger between the eyes. A loud popping noise cracked the sky as small fragments of skull splintered off. James stopped running when he saw the hole in the gunslinger's head.

The gunslinger paused. He stared at James and stood his ground. Both combatants stopped as they tried to figure out what would happen next. The gunslinger stuck his left pistol back in his holster. He reached up and felt around the crooked hole that stood out in the center of his forehead. James didn't see any blood leaking from the wound. The gunslinger poked his bony finger inside the hole, rimming the bone in a circular fashion. Then he removed the finger to inspect the tip for blood or brains. Something.

There was nothing. While the bullet seemed to damage the integrity of the gunslinger's head, it didn't do anything to put the ghost down. James thought he had a chance using this alternate strategy. Apparently not, he thought to himself.

The gunslinger started to laugh. He laughed hard, resting his bony hand upon his belly. The sickening gurgles of laughter prickled the skin on James' forearms. James watched motionless. Stunned. What else could he do? If bullets had no effect, then hitting the gunslinger wouldn't do anything either. James felt dejection wash over his body as the end seemed near. The gunslinger would kill him now, like it did Sheriff Morgan. Their bloodied bodies left to rot in the hot sunlight. Rodents and carrion feeding on the decaying remains. James imagined weeds growing through his rib cage, as his empty sockets looked to heaven.

The laughing slowly wound down as the gunslinger came back to the present. He took several steps toward James. The two, just feet apart, stared into each other's eyes. James tried to remain calm, but his body began trembling as it sensed its end. The gunslinger licked his lip-less mouth with a sickly tongue. He raised his six-shooter at James. The end of the barrel mere inches from James' chest.

"Make sure you say hello to your friends. Give my regards to Mayor Samuels and Sheriff Morgan."

James swallowed hard but leaned into the gun barrel. Defiance surged through his veins. He wasn't going to die without giving the gunslinger everything he had.

"I will. And I'll make sure Sally knows what her daddy has done."

CHAPTER 46

"What did you say to me?"

"That's right, boogiedman."

James and the gunslinger turned when the new voice spoke. It was Carson. The little boy stood off to the left of the camp fire. His upper body wrapped in dirty bandages. A greasy tuft of dirty blond hair poked off the side of his head. Dark circles rimmed beneath his eyes.

"What do we have here? The cavalry in town?"

Carson leafed through the small book with his good hand. He must have found it where James had dropped it. As he paged through the drawings, the gunslinger faced the boy. He moved in the direction of Carson before pausing.

"Gimme that book." The gunslinger spoke with a quaver in his voice.

"No."

"Gimme the book."

"No." Carson removed the old photograph from the inner cover. He had to wedge the book against his hip with his bandaged arm in order to get to it. The book fell to his feet. Carson rubbed some excess dust from the photo with his small finger. "She's pretty."

The gunslinger took a few more steps toward Carson. James caught another whimper from the ghost. He followed close behind the gunslinger.

"She was my whole life."

Carson squinted up at the gunslinger. Then he looked back at the photo. "I couldn't live without her."

James wondered how Carson had changed the gunslinger's emotions. Was it because he was a child, like Sally? Did Carson's slowness remind the gunslinger of his own daughter's disability? Or was it the purity? The innocence? Perhaps the absence of sin? Whatever the reason, James needed to take advantage of this opportunity.

The gunslinger knelt down and picked up the book. He turned it over in his hands, each finger tracing the fabric, attempting to connect with the original owner. He opened the book and stared at the first drawing. A shaky, bony finger traced some of the lines. The gunslinger looked up at Carson.

"She was special. Like you." The sounds came out in whispers. Sad and faint.

Carson handed the photograph to the gunslinger. His arm holding the faded picture in front of the apparition's face. The gunslinger accepted the photograph, caressing the faces that were captured in a brief moment in time. The gunslinger lowered his head and sobbed. Carson looked up at James and shrugged. James didn't understand if Carson was showing he didn't care or he didn't know what to do next.

Carson put his good hand on the gunslinger's shoulder. "It's okay."

The gunslinger stopped sobbing and looked at Carson. "I'm so sorry I hurt you."

Carson nodded. "You were just mad. I know you don't want to hurt me."

James was stunned. Was Carson going to forgive the gunslinger? After all of his pain and suffering? Is that all it would take to rid the haunting?

The gunslinger clutched Carson's shoulders. It looked like he searched Carson's eyes for something.

James realized the gunslinger had become a solid being. It dawned on him that Carson had patted the gunslinger's shoulder. And now the gunslinger was holding Carson. James felt an urge to rub his eyes to make sure he wasn't imagining things. It wouldn't surprise him if his mind were playing tricks on him. After all, the whole concept of haunted spirits shooting people was crazy. Maybe he was losing his mind.

"Why?"

The ghost of Doddy shook Carson as he bellowed to heaven.

"Why? Why? Why?"

Carson flopped like a rag doll in the clutches of the gunslinger. His face grew pale as the pain of the apparition's hands on his wounded arm washed over him.

James acted immediately. He spun the pistol around in his hand and hammered the handle upon the gunslinger's skull. The blow crunched bone beneath the flattened hat. James felt the recoil of connecting with a physical surface all the way up his arm.

The gunslinger tumbled to the dirt, dropping Carson. His hat flew from his head, revealing decayed sinews hidden beneath sparse crops of grayed hairs. A flap of loose flesh dangled from the back of his rotten scalp.

Before James could hammer another blow, the prone gunslinger kicked a spurred boot, connecting with James' face. The spur sliced through James' cheek, releasing a fountain of blood. He flew back against a burned out post. His gun lost in the shuffle.

The gunslinger regained his feet and charged James. A boot stomp crushed the wind out of him. The spur again removing gore. This time a chunk of meat tore from James' chest.

The ghost of Doddy lifted James off the ground by his throat. He struggled for air as he looked down into the crooked maw of the gunslinger. The black eyes narrowed with focus. He had to do something quick before he suffocated under the death grip.

James flailed his boots at the gunslinger. Each time they connected, the gunslinger seemed to hardly notice the strikes. It was like James' kicks were as weak as a gnat.

He used his right hand to throw a punch at the gunslinger. It glanced off the rotted skull as it grazed across the thin mustache and the bony nose. James attempted another swing but completely missed the second time around.

A loud crack thundered.

The gunslinger dropped James. He landed hard, what little air remained in his lungs escaped him.

From the ground, James saw Carson holding his gun. A wisp of smoke leaked from the barrel. Carson was crying. But he kept the gun trained on the tormentor.

The gunslinger looked down with shock. His bony fingers trying to hold in the spilling contents of his gut.

"You can't..."

Carson stared as tears ran down his cheeks. His expression revealed sadness. His posture, resolve.

"...kill me."

The gunslinger teetered to the side. His hands desperate to stuff back in his rotted innards. James gagged at the smells that carried on the soft breeze. He dragged himself to his feet, still doubled over and gasping for air.

Carson stood his ground as the gunslinger ambled toward him. The pistol aimed higher.

"Sally..."

BANG.

A hole cratered the gunslinger's forehead. His expression turned from sadness to surprise. The ghost of Doddy dropped to its knees and stared through Carson.

"I'm not Sally." Carson whispered.

The gunslinger fell forward and rolled on his side. Nothing leaked from the rounded hole in his forehead.

James climbed over the body, ready to finish the gunslinger off. But it was unnecessary. The ghost of Doddy was gone.

Carson handed James the pistol. He stuffed it in his belt loop and squeezed Carson to his chest. Carson squealed from the pain in his shoulder. James let go and apologized, messing Carson's hair.

"Carson!"

They both turned as Sarah came running through the desolation. She slid on her knees to embrace James and Carson. The three of them lost in the moment. Relieved that they were all alive. And still together.

Carson wriggled free and picked up the tattered book. He tucked it inside the gunslinger's duster, alongside the old photograph.

"What was that?" Sarah looked at James.

"A gift from the past."

Carson turned his face up to Sarah and James. "So he could show it to Sally."

Before Sarah could ask who Sally was, the shape of the gunslinger faded into the dust. Where there was once a corpse, only earth remained.

CHAPTER 47

James decided that they should wait until morning light to head back to town. He maintained the fire while the three of them sat huddled together. Carson spent most of the time balled up in Sarah's lap.

When the sun rose, James loaded Sheriff Axl Morgan's body across his horse. He tied the reins to his saddle so the horse would follow along. Carson and his mother rode together on the horse she had borrowed.

"What are we going to tell folks?" Sarah asked her question without looking at James.

"The truth."

"And what the hell would that be?"

James didn't know. He struggled to make sense of what had happened, let alone figure out how to explain it to someone else. Sheriff Morgan's death and his own wounds ought to give folks a rough idea of how bad things had gone. Although, they should be relieved the haunted gunslinger had now become a scary tale instead of an annual horror show.

Carson slouched in the saddle as he bounced upon Sarah's chest. James was worried about Carson. He had been through so much. Shot twice. Found out his mother was dead. And then he had to kill the gunslinger to save James. Since last night, he hadn't uttered a word. James recognized the far-off stare in Carson's eyes. The trauma of what had happened not completely understood by the young boy.

James touched the wound on his face and winced at the sharp pain. The cut from the gunslinger's spur was deep. He knew Doc Stinson would need to run some thread through it. And it would probably leave a scar. James furrowed his brow. The thought of a nasty scar on his face, affecting his chances of finding a beautiful woman someday, irked him. But at least he was alive, he reasoned.

As they rode slowly through the overgrown trail, James wondered what was next. He had lost his job at Miller's. And he didn't want to go back to sweeping up saloons. So his future was uncertain. Then James smiled. Uncertainty just meant that his calendar was wide open. He was free to figure out where to go and what to do. Maybe the town would hire him on as the new sheriff now. Nah, he thought. They would never choose a young man for the job. Besides, as much as he wanted to follow in Wyatt Earp's footsteps, serving as sheriff of one small town seemed too…well, small.

Carson glanced at James with sullen eyes. He was wrapped in a wool blanket even though the day's heat was rising already. James smiled at Carson, but the boy just turned his head back to the trail. No recognition of the eye contact whatsoever. James sighed. The worst scar left by the gunslinger would be his effect on Carson.

The town's edges came into view. James tugged the reins to stop the horses. His mother stopped alongside him. They stared at the town for a few long moments before turning to each other.

"I'm scared."

"Of what, sweetheart?"

"Them."

"Why?"

"I'm bringing back their dead sheriff." He touched his cheek. "And nobody likes me."

"He was OUR sheriff. And nobody knows you. So how could they judge you?"

"The Sheriff told me everyone blamed me for the Mayor's death. That I was the reason people were dying now."

"Oh, yeah? And how many of these folks stood toe to toe with the gunslinger? Huh? Which ones came out to the farm with you and the Sheriff to end it?"

James saw her point but he wasn't buying it. He knew they would tie him up and hang him once he rode in with the late sheriff.

"Besides, you afraid of some drunks and chicken shits?"

James swung to look at his mother. She rarely cussed but, when she did, it was usually something to remember. His face revealed his shock at her statement. Then it slowly turned into a grin.

She laughed. Just a few chuckles at first. Then she snorted through her nose, which turned the chuckles into downright laughter. James joined in, relief washing through him. She was right. He had fought Crouching Bear and the haunted gunslinger. What could these folks possibly do to him?

Carson's face switched between James and Sarah. He cracked a small smile. But he didn't laugh. James noticed. His laughter slowly settled down.

"Best be on our way then." He winked at his mother.

"Yep." She winked back.

James tugged the reins and they continued in the direction of the clock tower. He knew there would be questions and lots of shouting. He envisioned the whispers in the crowd drawing more folks from the shops and offices. Mobs growing around them. No room to move or breathe. Better to get it over with rather than delay it. Experiencing the mob could only happen once. In his head, it happened countless times.

His thoughts shifted to Eleanor as they neared the town. Their last encounter had been uncomfortable. He hoped he could make amends with her. Eleanor had been one of the few people who didn't despise James before. It would be real nice if they could get along like they had. He enjoyed his time with her. And he thought she was really pretty too. James wondered if a grown woman like Eleanor could ever be interested in a guy like him. Then again, even if she could, James got the not-so-subtle sense from his mother that she wouldn't approve of him spending time with her. James rolled his eyes to himself and grinned. Maybe there were more things about growing up that he had to learn. And he looked forward to it.

CHAPTER 48

"Here's to our new hero!"
"Here, here!"
"Well, down it, son."

James felt boxed in. The saloon was packed full of people and they all pressed in to get closer to him. He kept getting rough slaps on his back and punches to the shoulder. The town found cause for celebration in his return. And they wanted to drink to that.

More like the town never really needed a reason to celebrate so much as an excuse. But James wanted nothing to do with it. He was carried into the saloon on shoulders of men he had never seen before. At one point, he thought he had wandered into the wrong town because all the faces that came at him were those belonging to strangers. Until he caught glimpses of Mr. Miller and Clip Jones and several other town regulars.

The crowd pressed closer as they implored him to drink with them. The mob chanted, "Drink! Drink! Drink!" over and over again. James spun in circles, trying to search for his mother and Carson. Instead, he found a sea of dirty mustaches and tobacco stained teeth.

Panic ran through his veins until he realized the only way out of this situation was to knock back the whiskey they had handed him.

James downed the amber liquid.

And it burned.

James choked and coughed, gasping for air. His wheezing sent the crowd into an uproar, as even more hands smacked his back through the leather and denim waves. It felt like his eyes were going to shoot out of their sockets. Fire burned in his throat and gut. But then a nice warm calm spread to his extremities. The pain of the nasty firewater receded and left him somewhat…happy.

Another round was called for and rough hands pounded the bar in agreement. James noticed that the men nearest him were busy shouting into each other's faces about the ghost being dismissed. He saw his chance and began to wriggle through a few sturdy shoulders until he hit a brick wall. Not an actual brick wall. It was Sully. The man only went by one name, his nickname. Sully obviously stood for Sullivan which was his last name. His first name was Horace. But everyone in town knew not to call him by his Christian name unless you wanted to spend the rest of the afternoon searching for your teeth on the ground. Sully was part of the lumberyard gang. And he was HUGE.

"Going somewhere?"

"Me? No. I just, um…was, uh…"

Before James could finish stammering a lame excuse, Ed Miller squeezed past several men. He clapped Sully on the shoulder and beamed at James.

"James! My wonderful stock boy. You're a hero!"

James could smell the whiskey floating from Mr. Miller's breath.

"Mr. Miller? Have you been drinking?"

"Well, just one. And then another one. And another one." He cackled in James' face.

"I'm not your stock boy anymore. You fired me. Remember?"

"James, James, James. I didn't really fire you. I…gave you time off to slay the gunslinger. And you did it, my fine lad!"

"I don't know…"

"Think of the sales, James. Why, do you know how many people will come through our doors just to meet the fine savior of this town? Think, James. Each one buying more items just to be near you. We'll be rich!"

James waved the whiskey breath away with his hand. "I don't think folks will buy more soap just because of me."

Ed Miller furrowed his brow and nodded. "You may be right, James. But we can dream, can't we?" He leaned his head in and then started laughing. Each laugh bringing more water to James' eyes.

James chuckled and nodded.

The crowd shifted and Mr. Miller went away. James took the opportunity and started to burrow between men. His head was swimming a bit and his stomach pleaded for food.

Then he hit the wall again.

Sully shoved James to the front of the bar. A new round of back slaps and cheers. Someone started up a chorus of songs about James being a jolly good fellow. But the sounds morphed into an echoing din in his head. The room twisted and turned and it felt like the ground was moving beneath his boots. A shot glass, with amber liquid spilling over, slid in front of him. Sully's enormous hand placed the shot in James' and the whole room raised glasses to the ceiling. Then someone yelled "Up yer arse" and the crowd downed the whiskey.

Including James.

Suddenly, the pain in his cheek and chest disappeared. His exhaustion slipped away too. He wanted to dance for some reason. But he really didn't know how. It didn't matter though. Two women from the brothel upstairs were pushed into James. They were laughing and caressing his face. One of the ladies took off his hat and placed it on her head. Then the women squeezed James in the middle and attempted to dance around him. James laughed and clapped as another shot of whiskey found its way through the crowd. Without prompting, James downed the shot and threw the glass across the bar. He linked arms with the two ladies and a small circle of space spread around the threesome.

They danced and laughed. The mob clapped and cheered.

All thoughts of death and ghosts were absent.

As James enjoyed the alcohol-induced fervor, Sarah stood at the doorway. Her arms were folded across her chest. A stern expression painted her face as her crystal-blue eyes turned to ice. Her foot tapped the wooden floor, revealing her disapproval of James' behavior. And the town's goading.

She glanced down at Carson, who was still wrapped in the wool blanket. His expression was blank as he tried to watch the dance through the crowd. He looked up at Sarah. Then he shrugged.

Sarah smiled. And started to laugh. She must have figured there was nothing she could do at this point to get back her son. Sarah put her arm around Carson and they worked their way to the stairs.

And James danced on.

CHAPTER 49

James vomited.

Again.

Doc Stinson nodded to the nurse to remove the chamber pot. The frustration was evident on the doctor's face. He was trying to stitch James' cheek together. But they had had to stop so James could get sick. Twice. The string dangled from James' face while he hung off the cot.

It had been a long night. James partied into the wee hours. Until Sully carried him upstairs to their room like a small child. Sarah had laughed when she saw James hanging around Sully's neck while passed out.

Now James was experiencing his first hangover. His head inflated against the band of his hat. His temples throbbed and his stomach felt like he had swallowed dirty horse trough water. Any slight movement seemed like the whole world was shaking. He did not feel well.

"Sit still, James." Doc Stinson huffed, as he tried to continue stitching.

"Uhhhhhhh." James moaned instead of telling Doc Stinson what he really felt like saying. IF he could actually form a sentence.

James squinted. Not from the thread sliding through his wound, but from the bright light shining in the windows of the hospital. James thought he was on the sun, between the heat and the brightness.

"Guess his first night out with the boys didn't end well."

"What gave you that impression, Doc?" His mother's sarcasm burned through him but his head hurt too much to fight it.

"Boys will be boys."

"Funny how that excuse works for the boys, but not the gals, huh?"

This time Doc Stinson shot Sarah a dirty look. Apparently he wasn't given to women's issues. Sarah grinned with contempt, regardless.

"There we go. Good as new. Well, almost."

James turned and vomited again. This time it splattered on the floor. The nurse hadn't made it back yet with the cleaned out chamber pot. Doc Stinson groaned at the mess in his office. Sarah folded her arms and nodded to James that it served him right. Carson wrinkled his tiny nose at the awful smell.

"At least the booze is coming out. It smells like it came straight outta the bottle." Doc Stinson stood to leave. "I suggest you lie down right where you are, young man. And ride this one out."

"Sounds good to me. I don't want that mess in my room." Sarah's sarcasm still overt.

James rolled over and stared at his mother. Right now he hated her guts. Because he knew she was right. He quietly swore to God that he would NEVER, EVER drink booze again. He didn't even like the taste of it. Although, he had had fun for a while last night. Nope. No more. That was one side of being a man that he didn't want to go through again.

The sound of heels clomped loudly on the floor. The noise pierced James' head like an iron bar being rammed between his eyes. He wished it would go away.

Eleanor Lark stormed past Sarah and Carson. She brushed Doc Stinson aside too.

"James. I have to say something to you. And you're going to listen to me."

Sarah looked at Carson and then followed along again.

"I know you think that I had something to do with keeping the secrets of the gunslinger from you. But I had no idea about the legend. These crummy people in this smelly town kept the secret from me too. And then you left town to fight the ghost without saying goodbye to me as if I didn't matter. And that just hurt me, James. It hurt me badly. And, as angry as I am at you, I don't want you to walk away without knowing how I feel about you. So here I go."

Eleanor stomped her foot down on the wooden floor and threw herself upon James. Her mouth enclosed James' and she kissed him hard. Deeply and hard. Her face puckered up as she tasted the flavor of sick in his mouth.

Sarah stifled a laugh with her hand. She looked down at Carson whose face was crunched up in disgust. Sarah noticed that Doc Stinson wore the same expression, as he rushed out of the room.

Eleanor sat up on the end of the cot. She touched her lips while her tongue ran around the inside of her mouth. She tried to hide the fact that she was sickened from kissing a freshly vomited mouth. But it didn't last. She turned and spewed over James' legs onto the floor. James watched her and then he began to retch. Then he hung his head over the same side of the cot and followed suit.

Sarah laughed out loud now. There seemed to be no need to hide the hilarity in the moment. Carson apparently didn't think any of it was funny. He folded his one good arm in front of his chest, imitating Sarah's displeased posture from earlier. Sarah noticed and thought it was so cute. She messed Carson's hair and told him she was heading home. Sarah left the room.

Carson just stared at James and Eleanor as they spasmed in unison. He shook his head in disgust and followed in Sarah's footsteps.

CHAPTER 50

James slammed the cards down. Carson had won again. James thought he had a chance to win since he got to shuffle today. With Carson's arm still bandaged up, James volunteered to handle the dealing responsibility. In the back of James' mind, Carson may have had the upper hand in the past because he controlled the cards from start to finish. But it didn't matter.

Carson smiled at James. "I told you to pay attention."

James ignored the taunt. He paid attention every time they played cards. He hated that Carson reminded him anyway.

His mother was working down the hall. It hadn't taken her long to get back to work after returning from the farm. She had girls to manage and customers to attend to. Money was money and Sarah wanted to make as much as she could.

They had debated last night whether they would stay here in Wichita or move on. So much had taken place in such a short period of time. And, while the townspeople seemed to be okay with James now that he removed the gunslinger, they still weren't sure if this was the right place to settle down. It might be a better idea to just pull up and head out to another location. A place that would provide them with another fresh start. Of course, they couldn't do anything until Carson healed.

"James, where are we going?"

"I don't know, buddy."

"But mommy and you was arguing last night. She said we could leave."

"We talked about possibilities, not actually leaving."

"But I don't want to stay here with Elnor."

"It's Eleanor. And why would we stay here with her?"

"You're in love with her. Mommy said so."

James smiled. He didn't know if he loved Eleanor. But he was definitely fond of her. He still couldn't believe that an older woman liked him. She gave him his first kiss, even if it made her puke afterward. He chuckled. It was kind of funny that he had made her sick on their first kiss.

"Eleanor is a good friend. You don't have to worry about her taking me away from you, pal. I'll always be with you."

"Maybe."

James read the hurt in his tone.

"I know I have lied to you in the past and left you behind. But I won't do it again. You saved my life, Carson. I'll never forget that. You're my hero."

Carson looked up at James with a serious expression. Then he cracked a little smirk of approval.

"I need you when I fight the bad guys. We are a team now. Just like we always dreamed about."

Carson smiled wider. "Okay. Deal again."

"Do we have to play another game? Can't we just talk or something?"

"Talkin' is for cowards. Deal."

Carson slapped his good hand on the table. James rolled his eyes and sighed. He went about shuffling the deck several times to ensure a good mix. James dealt the cards. They both inspected their hands. Carson's face was stoic. James raised an eyebrow as he studied his cards. He thought he might have him this time.

James laid his hand down. Two aces over two kings. He beamed down at Carson. "Beat that!"

Carson's tongue squirmed out and he tilted his head. He slowly laid his cards down over James'. A straight flush.

James rocked back in his chair. He let out a slow whistle. Carson grinned. James threw the cards back into the pile.

"Back to square one." James admitted defeat.

"Hey!" Carson protested vehemently.

James started laughing.

DIRECTOR'S CUT

So what did you think of the second installment?
    I love these characters. They feel so real to me. Not that the characters in any of the other stories I write don't. But I am definitely drawn to James and Sarah and Carson.

I've been told not to write these books because they probably won't sell. Western Horror is a minuscule, niche genre with fickle readers. And I respond, "So what." These characters need to live and their stories need to be told. Plain and simple. If I only wrote what would sell, then you would find a lot more romantic-zombie-thriller-erotica titles under my name.

And I am not alone.

I met fellow authors, Gary Jonas and Sam Witt in Austin, Texas. Both writers have shown faith in the Western Horror genre with the Night Marshal Series and the Pitchfork County Series, respectively. Then I met Jonathan Janz and Kristopher Rufty in Williamsburg, Virginia. Janz's novel, Dust Devils, and Rufty's novel, Seven Buried Hill, are two more examples of fun Western Horror stories. And do I need to mention Joe R. Lansdale or Stephen King? You might want to check their back catalogs for related stories.

So where are you going with this, Mr. Buda?

Not sure. But the stories are there for a reason. Because they need to be told. And you need to read them. What better mash-up could there be than Western and Horror? Some prefer Cowboys and Aliens but I don't. I did enjoy the movie but the Old West was scary as it was. Folks trying to carve out a new life for their families. Against the terrain, the elements, the natives and each other. Now sprinkle in some vampires or demons or even zombies. And you've got something scary.

Sarah and Carson were developed more in this book. I had plans for them to become more integral from the beginning but I figured it would be too much for the first book. James had to establish himself as the lead character before I could complicate the tales. Of course, we've now seen James mature more too. He is finally realizing that the glorious life of a media hero ain't all it's cracked up to be. People start to peck away at him when he gets more exposure. They second guess his choices and pass judgment without walking a mile in his boots. Sounds familiar to many present-day stories, no?

Well, pull up yer britches and hold on to yer hat because the next story is going to get crazy. I have more in store for James and Carson. Things are about to get a whole lot more complicated.

I hope you enjoyed reading The Haunted Gunslinger. And, if you haven't read Curse of the Ancients, then you have about two months to go grab a copy and catch yourself up. The West is gonna get wild. YEEHAW!

Chuck Buda

P.S. I hope you will join us in Book 3 to find out what lurks beneath the tombstones.

I feel safer with you by my side.

ABOUT THE AUTHOR

Chuck Buda explores the darkest aspects of the human condition. Then he captures its essence for fictional use. He writes during the day and wanders aimlessly all night…alone.

Chuck Buda co-hosts The Mando Method Podcast on Project Entertainment Network with author, Armand Rosamilia. They talk about all aspects of writing. Subscribe so you don't miss an episode. You can find The Mando Method Podcast on iTunes, Stitcher and most other places where podcasts are available. Or you can listen directly from the Project Entertainment Network website.

www.PROJECTENTERTAINMENTNETWORK.com

CPSIA information can be obtained
at www.ICGtesting.com
Printed in the USA
BVHW051134281122
652924BV00009B/172